For

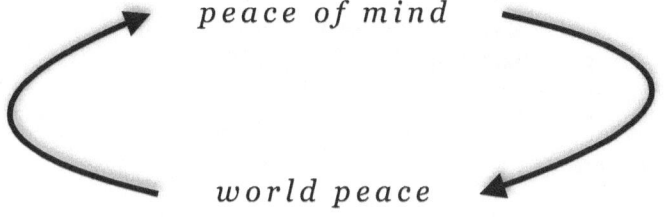

peace of mind

world peace

MI1.club
New York
ISBN: 979-8-9877558-0-8
Library of Congress Control Number: 2024910964

A STORY
ABOUT TWO TRUTHS AND PICKLED WATERMELONS

THEY SAID IT'S TRUE

MILA ILKOVA

Media Never Lies

New York

MIRRA VLADI SERIES

Mirra Vladi's adventures from dating in New York City to accidentally causing a revolution, from solving a world crisis to pickling watermelons, from raising kids to finding love in all its forms. In other words, well, life.

BOOK 1. NEW YORKERS HATE FOOD

In New York City, where relationships last no longer than an H&M T-shirt, Mirra navigates the messy online dating scene with a barrage of men, like a homeless millionaire, a perfect bicep bro, an overly interested in casual sex prince, and an alarmingly interested in immediate marriage creep. And then, Mirra meets Sunshine only to discover that love, besides all, can also be an addiction. If only there were a rehab for that.

BOOK 2. TEN MYRIAD MOVES

With only a thousand dollars and an existential crisis, Mirra Vladi manages to buy property in Big Sur, write and sell a movie script, found an international company, and cause a state revolution. But the latter is totally by accident.

BOOK 3. THEY SAID IT'S TRUE

A group of Americans decides to restore justice and create a crisis in Russia by messing up with their national strategic reserve—kasha. But the greater power intrudes. No, not nuclear power—the power of truth.

DON'T THINK ABOUT IT

I am sitting in the office with my ripped pants off, bare ass on the chair, papers scattered all over the floor, and everything is falling apart. How on Earth did I end up with an office job again?! And with a rubber hot water bottle, vibrator, and toilet brush in the desk drawer.

Two years ago, I became the head of the strategic analytics department at Star Democracy Freedom Group (SDFG), covering all things information. They found me and made an offer, and thank god because it saved me a lot of time on sending out resumes and fan fiction about working at their companies, a.k.a. cover letters. SDFG let me hire my team and have a lot of freedom, as much freedom as one can get working for the main client—the state. Well, deep state. SDFG is a consulting firm. Neither right nor left, neither right nor wrong, neither pro nor against, neither we nor they, neither here nor there, neither this nor that. Those terms and categories don't exist in their world. It is independent of all political agendas and is ruling all of them at the same time. Even I had no idea how deep it goes. Yet, here I am: paycheck to paycheck, a very good one though, analyzing this, analyzing that but not analyzing anything beyond. The unofficial slogan is "Stop thinking and think about it".

If an organization, profit or nonprofit, has the word freedom or democracy in its title, do know that someone is curating it. However, these days it's easier to tell which organizations are not being curated. Thus, all kinds of conspiracy theories form. Quite a few of them aren't far from the truth, frankly. But my job is to strategize and analyze; others tell. The firm is ahead of those who are ahead of anything. I mean, the firm forms anything.

Geopolitics is way more complicated than one thinks. Everyone's a product of the information flows they live in. Here's an example on a local level: a Democrat can easily be turned into a Republican and vice versa just by putting them into the corresponding information environment and blocking the opposing opinion, plus the social group pressure. If there was a grant for PhD research like that available, I'd totally win it. The sameness of news on every channel, in each paper, on all stations, and in socials creates the same effect, mesmerizing the audience for a certain opinion. One chunk of the target audience is prone to gullibility, and another good chunk is dunce. It wouldn't take long. An example on the world level would be changing regimes.

All it takes to put any idea into any head is the selection of information, the totality of information, like-mindedness, and the communication system. Then mix it with a tendency to be easily persuaded that something is true or real, name it big and significant that's, by definition, unprovable value hard to measure—like freedom of speech—and assign value to it. Ta-da! Done. It is impossible to prove what doesn't exist. Freedom of speech is not just about talking—it's also about listening. The government doesn't listen to slaves. Freedom of speech is slaves have high-speed internet access and a choice out of two. If you have a choice out of two options—you have no choice. Freedom from choice?

Freedom today is to say what's allowed. Humans aren't born with a default setting of opinions and prejudices. Those are all formed by society, advertising, and propaganda. No, you don't think that Cola-Cola is better than Pepsi. That idea was put in your head through genius strategic content.

Already now, like in the Black Mirror, constant content interrupts thoughts and does not allow you to think, neither critically nor at all, from which the brain turns into an over-steamed dumpling. It is easier to control the consciousness of the masses that way. Cognitive sovereignty is not convenient.

There's so much content that we must use headphones to block the incoming noise, but then we have the noise from the headphones and our inner voice, unknown which one is louder. Thus, the noise is constant and unavoidable. Then we get used to constantly blocking it, which leads to not hearing the important.

Because of so much content today, soon enough people will start to lose their ability for imagination.

Now, people compete in what they know—knowledge and skills prevail. With AI development, the only skill people will be competing in is how to operate an AI. And then, for security purposes, please let it know you're a human. The Human Element sounds like a great name for AI.

Yeah, there are a lot of tech dorks who can't communicate properly but decide algorithms and what we should think about anything. Oh, I'm sorry. Is there another word for dorks invented this year so dorks don't get offended for being dorks?

Containers for food and shit is where our life is headed. We must value markets. They will soon disappear because everything is evolving, and a farmer with artificial intelligence instead of manure sounds like a joke.

In the future, the implanted chips into anuses will connect to our smartphones. To pay for goods and services—sit on a merchant's stake a little. Now, it's the same type of torture but called online accounts.

Technology creates the problems that technology solves. With AI gaining more and more popularity and people being thrilled about how you don't have to think anymore, an algorithm can do it for you instead... I'm just going to do what I can until I can't.

I used to consume content to interrupt my thoughts. Now, on the contrary, I turn off all content to think and analyze the content I just consumed and strategize the next steps for using it. The choice is the hardest.

Daily, I have to consume lots of propaganda from all mediums worldwide. Politically correct word: news. Absolutely all of them are propaganda. Objectivity is not a thing when it comes to news. There's no truth—there's narrative. Each country has its own, especially the most democratic one. I know! Mindblower.

Here's how it works: you can do pro and against anything, depending on the narrative and what you want to use the tool for.

Marijuana: promote the usage if you want people to stop thinking critically. To increase thinking critically promote education.

Reduce birth and population: transgender and gay rights. Increase birth and population: ban abortion. Soon enough, there will be a reality show: pregnant women vs transgender wars. They always call it wars in the reality TV world. Or, as an alternative, pay mothers for giving birth, more and more for each kid respectively, and call it state maternity capital. They only care about women's rights when she's a fetus. So why waste state funds when church and independent fanatics can just shame women for being fetus murderers? Women can take it. Ministry of Women, Diversity and Compote will take care of it by putting the magic serum on shelves for eighty-nine ninety-nine to hide the stress off of their faces.

Be reelected president: reduce the gas price (or at least keep it as is, not higher), call your opponent fascist and form a National Commission on Freedom of Speech and Development of Information Industry to filter mass information, find an external enemy that is greater than current internal problems—not necessarily in that order.

Parliament, as a live group chat, is not a place for discussions. Real decisions are made elsewhere. There are players and there are artists.

Group chats are nonsense. That is why I am not in

any group chat except work because that one is required. One goat texts "Have a good weekend" and then the rest of the goats text back "Thank you, you too" and you get notifications like thirty times in a row. Stop it, people! Stop it, stop it, stop it! In a personal meeting, people don't repeat the same thing over and over again. So, stop it!

I log into Teams for a scheduled group call and receive seventeen notifications that all say "morning" in the group chat. Ugh!

"Hi, team," the Senior Vice President of Who-Gives-a-Shit waves onto the screen. "Happy Monday!" he smirks. "I hope you had a good weekend because Russia is out of hand again, so it looks like we all will be working this week a lot," the Senior Vice President of Who-Gives-a-Shit continues.

"What did they do now?" the Director of Sweat and Tears Operations asks.

"Democracy is on the line. They are becoming so successful again that it might be a threat to our international policy. Besides, they are helping the government of THE COUNTRY that we claim is living in dictatorship by interfering in their election process."

"Again? Oh no! I was supposed to fly to the Bahamas with my wife this weekend," the Regional Manager of Whoop-dee-do says.

"Is there a legit proof?" I ask.

"Our statement should be enough. Period," the Senior Vice President of Who-Gives-a-Shit says.

"What country is it?" the Director of Sweat and Tears Operations asks.

"THE COUNTRY. It is a top-secret country that we

can't announce on Teams, team. But I assure you it's somewhere there on the map," the Senior Vice President of Who-Gives-a-Shit says.

Isn't Russia an independent and sovereign federation? Why does America always need to be in charge and hunt Russia down and not let it do anything? Russia doesn't do this to America. Does America really have to be the world gendarme all the time? When something happens to America, Russia doesn't give a damn, but how America pries "sincerely" worrying about Russia is bravo.

Of course, I keep things like these to myself. Over time I've learned how to ask questions silently because most of them aren't mainstream accepted opinions hence problems can arise at any given moment; and you never know how, in what way, and when your words will be used against you. Just like in the Miranda warning given by police: whatever you say will be used against you.

I tried to open a controversy tab, thinking I could find something controversial, but access was denied.

One can consider oneself an expert in digital forensics, but some government agencies have access to data recovery tools that even tech guys don't have. That being the case, it's best to practice political correctness when sending something questionable. Don't write something that you'll be sorry for later if someone brings it up to you. That being said, it is impossible to know what kind of a time bomb will explode depending on trending correctness yesterday, today, and tomorrow. Inclusivity and equality for all: humans, flora, fauna, and a woman-dental technician.

The modern version of socialism at its worst.

Ironically, based on total equality, soviet communism was created.

Liberalism is very totalitarian. Animals are not so cruel. Only people are truly cruel.

People are never killed for lying, only for telling the truth.

We are moving towards a commune where we will all look the same, dress the same, speak the same, identify the same—faceless, nomadic creature with no roots, history, culture; and god forbid you dare to express an extreme statement or think the wrong thing. Immediately, you will be pressured to feel sorry for being who you are if you remember your roots, history, and culture. The database system forgets to check the DNA test results—that algorithm just isn't there. Globalism, like a pandemic, shuts everyone in—into the only acceptable norm. Ridiculous democratorship.

The world is much more interesting with different civilizations, and the intersection of cultures yields very important results for humankind. True universalism takes the best from all. And yet...

In a country with freedom of speech and democracy and human rights, I noticed, no one expresses their opinion openly and publicly, because they are afraid. Especially today, you need to be careful when there is a system of analysis and control of communication, and any careless word can be decisive. You're more shut in the "truth" world than anywhere else, ever. Welcome to the democratic society 2.0. where mainstream equals propaganda, snitching is appreciated, and too much free speech can be silenced for good.

Free...aha, pun intended. I can't do it like that—I ask uncomfortable questions.

"...that is why we need to destroy Russia and their dictator and obliterate it from the world's minds!" the Senior Vice President of Who-Gives-a-Shit concludes.

Wait, what?! I look at the laptop screen in bewilderment. *First of all, dictator? That's hilarious. And destroy? Didn't you guys learn anything from me when I tried to educate you on Russian mentality and habits and what had happened in their history and where they are headed on the geopolitical map? Did you learn zilch? Has my meticulous analytics on everything and anything Russian been for nothing for the past two years? You should've listened to Mirrachka, when I tried to replace your destructive martial law state of mind into productive sunshine state of mind so all would be happy. But no! Some want to color their sunshine bloody red! Ugh.*

The United States can create problems better than others. But world domination requires solving problems, not creating them. A typical approach to "inconvenient, non-obedient" countries is rampant divide and conquer, tear them apart and see what they'll do to each other. No level of coolness can compensate assholeness in any form. It all starts with one person doing one annoying thing, then there's a group of people doing it, then a community, a city, a country, and then a whole world is full of assholes. Is that the world you want to live in?

It's a little funny to think you're superior, especially when you don't know much about the rest of the world. Illiteracy is a guarantee of democracy. One essential thing to know: if your country is rich in natural resources, it becomes a threat to the national security of the United States.

The hegemon does not produce anything except rotten democracy and imports it to other countries that don't have it. Other countries are not asked though whether they want it or not. They just get it through javelins and stingers; and information wars.

Any weapon, if it exists, will be used sooner or later. And the law forbidding it simply does not exist.

In the name of peace, wars are started.

In the name of democracy, nations are destroyed.

In the name of prosperity, robberies are done.

You can put everyone else down and be better this way or you can honestly be better. Who's interested in honesty when power is at stake?

The media flywheel and deep fake maker are running at full speed, depicting characters, conveying policy agendas, sticking narrative right into your face.

Regardless of the category, the story has to be challenging enough to advance the public conversation. Resonate, resonate, resonate. Shock, scare, empathize, decide, and make conclusions for the audience, not giving a slight chance for critical thinking. Legalize weed, ban abortion, start wars (pardon, spread democracy). Kill, kill, kill. Shock, scare, report. If it's on the media—it's true. You've seen videos with your own eyes, you've heard people screaming at top of their lungs with your own ears. You trust that, because why wouldn't you, right? Even if the news are fake, your emotions are always real.

Constant bad news takes away sleep, then a smile,

then a sense of security. Collective trauma. Within time you get used to that and become a senseless asshole—a defensive mechanism of your mind. It's like your inner world closes to the outer world—you become numb, only until something else horrible comes up. There's another extreme response to all that—everyone's good manners have gone. The combination of inflation, mass shootings, climate-related disasters, and political polarization has taxed our capacity to cope. Constant bad news causes a collapse in civility.

Emotional pictures and absurdism are the main elements of news content in mass media, separately for the regular evening news or together in one story for breaking news. It's like when a refugee crisis happened and people in old plaid shirts hitched a ride on armored personnel carriers. Then an outlet store gave humanitarian aid and a car rental company gave limos because there was a shortage of transportation. Poor people, in Gucci outfits, were being transported in limos—a very typical refugee situation. It was not on the news because the world would laugh at the absurdity of it and the desired emotional response was supposed to be different.

The media broadcasts what's convenient for its government today. Who's the good guy and who's the bad guy? Is it the absolute value or do they rotate their titles? The number of villains in the modern world has exceeded all sanitary standards. The President. Which one? The Dictator. Which one? Ask the Book of Wonder. The real question is: who are we screwing up this time?

Society is divided into rich and poor but not in a

primitive who's got more money sense. When the media has compromising data on somebody, and they have data on everybody, only the rich can use their money to silence the media and stop the story from going public.

It's all PR: it's all just fucking PR! Pay to cause black PR to someone, and then pay extra so that they stop atrociously screwing around. After a while, the media may get excited so much that it disgraces by inertia. By inertia, there is no desire to disgrace Russia at all. None of it is fair.

Everything in the information space is manipulation—creating circumstances and events that later seem accidental.

Like George Carlin said, "The media are almost literally exploding with bullshit! 'Cause they're located right at the crossroads of all the other bullshit! The media are made up of equal parts: advertising, politics, business, public relations, and show business. These people are sitting right at the bullshit junction!"

Repeated phony information causes mutilation of outlook on life. Influenced by the media, people join the mass opinion because it's easier that way. They receive their order and go to execute. Bullshit & Associates LLC. People trust those who fill the information space. Silver lining: to be brainwashed, you've got to have a brain to begin with. As Abraham Lincoln said, "You can fool some of the people all of the time and all of the people some of the time, but you can not fool all of the people all of the time."

All you need to do is go beyond the boundaries of the information space. As soon as you step outside its framework, which usually coincides with the state borders, you are surprised that there is another life, different from the nonsensical problems: people there worry about what lipstick to buy for the upcoming season, and not how to install multiple launch rocket system.

Going beyond the borders might mean living a little brighter and then subside again into the humus of the main ideology. One might refuse to go back and support that ideology; and when a lot of people don't support something, that becomes their new ideology. They immediately want you to answer all their questions because they need answers about your ideology. They want to know who you are and press you to know who you are, too. Abstaining is not enough. Still, I remember the times when asking for someone's political views was considered mauve ton. Decorative democracy, no matter how you look at it. Changing your ideology, your opinion is like looking at Tom Cruise who's been twenty-five for the past fifty years, and then suddenly his face is saggy.

True freedom is freedom from the influence, in one place or another. But is it even possible?

Literally, nothing has changed since almost a century ago:

> The press does not tolerate gaps in its information and works without skimping. For a seed to germinate, nature throws many seeds into the wind. The press does the same. It picks up and spreads rumors, multiplying them endlessly. Hundreds and thousands of

messages die out until a reliable version becomes stronger. Sometimes this happens only after a number of years. But it also happens that there is no time for truth at all.

What is striking in all those cases where public opinion is captured to the quick is human deceit. I speak about this without any moral indignation, rather in the tone of a natural scientist who is stating a fact. The need for lies, as well as the habit of lying, reflects the contradictions of our lives. We can say that newspapers tell the truth rather as an exception. I don't want to offend journalists with this. They are not very different from other people. They are their mouthpiece.

Zola wrote about the French financial press that it is divided into two groups: the corrupt and the so-called "incorruptible", that is, those that sell themselves in exceptional cases and at a very high price. Something similar can be said about the deceitfulness of newspapers in general. The yellow street press lies casually, without thinking or looking back. Newspapers, like the Times or the Temps, tell the truth in all indifferent and unimportant circumstances, in order to be able, in necessary cases, to deceive public opinion with all the necessary authority.

"My Life" by Leon Trotsky, 1930

Opening the News app and reading the news is

like: Okay, what am I doing wrong today? Am I well again? "At this point am I even breathing right?

Curated by the Ministry of Morons, the media creates news for morons.

Article headline 1: "How Worried Should You Be About Dying In Your Sleep?" *If you worry, you won't be able to sleep so don't worry about dying that's for sure.*

Article headline 2: "The Surprising Benefits of Negative Thinking. How seeing the glass as half-empty could actually transform your life for the better." *Oh, thank god! That constant positivity trend is toxic.*

Article headline 3: "New Program in Canada Gives Doctors the Option of Prescribing National Park Visits." *How much are Parks and Recreation lobbyists making for this?*

Article headline 4: "The Reason You're in a Better Mood After You Poop According To a Gastro. There's a connection between constipation and mood: a correlation between depressive and gastrointestinal disorders from the least happy when constipated to the happiest when not." *Yes, shit can make you feel shitty.*

Article headline 5: "Download RentCompare and We'll Tell You If You Overpay For Your Rent." *It's New York! Everyone overpays for their rent! No app is required to tell me that.*

The world is not as fucked up as it might seem when you scroll through the headlines.

Everyone is entitled to be stupid but some abuse the privilege, they say. I'd love to write a comedy movie in *Idiocracy* style how the world is divided into smarts and dumbs. One day dumbs decide to start the war against smarts... and lose it, well, because they are dumb. That's the only way fair.

Some people meditate to get fully in the moment. I sometimes don't know how to get out of the moment because I'm always so present.

Something's wrong. Something's deeply wrong. All of it. I don't know for sure what it is, but I know the feeling. My gut is screaming that it needs to be taken care of or else something majorly bad will happen. Change is coming. The most unpleasant wish is that you live in an era of change.

After the group chat, I close the laptop, get up from my office chair to come to the window and everything starts to fall apart. In complete solitude, I stumble upon literally nothing, land on my fours, and my pants rip in half on my butt. As I try to stand up, holding on to the desk, I hook the papers from the desk surface that scatter all over the floor, and on top of that, I knock over a cup of coffee that tips over my pants.

Sitting with my bare ass out makes me realize that a lot of things that might seem obvious aren't that at all. If anyone came to my office and saw me half-naked, their first thought would not be: "Oh, she must have topped coffee over herself." They would have thought something nasty, dirty, and inappropriate right away because this is how the human mind works. Give the mind some ambiguous information with a hint—assumptions will do the rest. Nothing is definite, obvious, or simple anymore; and there's nowhere to hide in the world because it's all the same

THEY SAID IT'S TRUE

globally.

They expect the "destroy Russia" strategy from me soon.

I've got to walk the decision out, and buy new pants.

Outside, as I walk, I notice a book in the bookstore window titled "Christ in Crisis". *If even Christ is in crisis then I don't know what we're hoping for.*

I see the homeless guy that I met a few times before near Macy's. He is now sitting near the Grand Central entrance on Vanderbilt Avenue—same tired face, same ripped coat. Even though he's a bum, there's something about him—something invisible is all over his face, like he doesn't belong here (not that anyone belongs to living in the street). The bum has a smart face, which you barely ever see. He doesn't scare me or make me abhor at all.

"Hey, man. You hungry?"

"Mirra! How is it going?"

Whoa. "How do you know my name?"

"You told me your name when you bought me chicken with broccoli a while ago near Macy's. I remember everyone who pays attention to me and everything they got me," he says and then adds: "I can always eat."

"What do you want?" I ask. Maybe he has a preference.

"I'd kill for a burrito right now. I mean I wouldn't "*kill*" kill, you know." He is a bit confused.

"You got it. Wait here," I say.

"Mirra, where would I go? To a nail salon?" he smirks.

One can never survive New York City without a sense of humor.

"What's your name, hun?" I ask.

"It's Ian," he answers.

I get him a juicy burrito at Chipotle. Ian eats it slowly, enjoying every single bite as if he were a regular at Cipriani across the street and held a membership at a golf club on Long Island.

"How did you end up here, if you don't mind me asking?" I am curious.

"I am here by mistake," he says. "My own mistake. Long story short: don't do drugs. They do ruin everything. Ironic enough, I was very good at calculating and trading on the futures market, but I couldn't calculate my own future on drugs."

"You're right. It is ironic," I say. "I now can't calculate my thing either. Maybe we can only calculate well if it doesn't concern us?"

"What are you trying to calculate?" he asks.

Am I really talking about it with a homeless guy? "I'm trying to calculate the odds of Russia going down, America keeping things as is, and the possibility of a nuclear war."

"Well, if you want my opinion..."

What the hell. Sure. Bring it on.

"A crisis on the market for buckwheat can be created because it's the basis of their economy, and if that goes to shit—the country goes to shit, angry and hungry people will eventually go out in the street and replace their leader through revolution. Typical scenario."

The worse life is, the more patriotism in society is

24

inflated. It's easier to live this way to replace necessities. "But?" I add. There's always a but.

"Other players need to want to set the price low as well. In case other players decline to support the decision and on the contrary lower the production—the price will go up caused by a shortage of supply and higher demand, it all might end up helping Russia boost their economy instead," he concludes.

Yeah, right. That sounds like a textbook on putting down Russia, silly. This has never happened before and here it is again. One thing not taken into consideration is Russian unpredictability, wittiness, and silly luck avos.

"How do you follow the news?" I ask.

"There's a bunch of TV screens in the window at PC Richards. They're on mute, but the subtitles are on, so I read. Plus newspapers at the public library, although most Manhattan branches don't let me in—based on my looks I don't seem to care about economics. I am homeless—I care about economics the most!"

"Do you miss work?" I ask.

"I miss work a lot! I miss being needed. Work was my everything even when I had everything: a beautiful wife, a big house, and a reputation. And then I lost everything," Ian says.

"Get up. Let's go get you a phone," I say.

"I'll most likely sell it in exchange for... you know. I need money, but I can't have it." He gets up, though.

"I know. We'll get you a burner so I can call you in case..."

"There's a case?" he interrupts me.

"Maybe. I don't know yet. Gotta calculate," I reply honestly.

He gets a flip phone. I love flip phones—if they made good ones these days, I'd buy one for myself.

"Now what?" he flips the phone open.

I call his number, so he has mine.

"I'll help you," I say.

"And in return, I'll need to...?" he pauses.

"Hopefully, you'll help me too," I finish.

"I told you, Mirra, I can't have money in my already-hit-the-bottom life—it'll literally kill me."

"Fine, you'll help me pro bono. A favor if you wish. Time to get up from the bottom and go up, hun!"

That coffee on my ripped pants might save the world because thanks to it I have a plan in mind. Okay, people! Let's incorporate the buckwheat plan to beat evil and identify who's actually the evil. It's only fair. And, if lucky, find an answer to the question: Why do humans that suck disproportionately affect the quality of the world for those of us that don't?

I call my husband Dylan.

"How is your day, baby?" Dylan asks.

"Looks like I'm going to be involved in a new project," I reply without any possible indication of mood.

"So happy for you. We should celebrate when you get back home."

"We should." Shit show down here, but now I am really glad I am involved."

"A good shit show is almost worth living for," Dylan says.

I laugh. He always makes me laugh.

"It's going to be either genius or terrible," I say.

"The project?"

"The outcome. Like in a joke: Pinocchio jerked off and set himself on fire."

"Did he survive the fire or fell asleep and burned?" Dylan asks.

"Unnecessary details," I say and hear him giggling. "Dylan, tomorrow first thing in the morning, we need to go tree-hugging to reunite with nature."

"Consider done." He doesn't ask me why—he loves my crazy, and nature.

The true beauty of a country house is how quickly you're able to simply relax.

In the world of crazy and chill, everything has to be balanced.

New York lives on the contrast and that is its balance.

I once saw a window ad that read: If you want to become a real New Yorker, there's only one rule—you have to believe New York is, has been, and always will be the greatest city on Earth. The center of the universe.

New York surely puts you on the spectrum of emotions.

You love it. You've seen it in movies, the lights are always magical. The walking and talking. Some move to New York for the sandwiches and a deli guy who yells if you don't know which sandwich you want. That is perceived by most people as rude but you know it's about saving time. And that's exactly why you love it. Get straight to the point.

You hate it. The dirt, the loudness, the rats, the

sirens. No one in this city can die quietly: everybody has to hear it! The city is like that crazy person who uses seven exclamation points in messages. With time you become indifferent to it and just don't care. It's worse than hate. Living in New York for almost a decade you don't even cry anymore when upset or frustrated. You just sigh and move on.

In New York the bigger the freak show the more okay you feel. The math theoretical formula: the further you are from Manhattan the happier you are. True or false? Both. The NYC paradox. City loyalty is like friendship: it needs time.

Your New York is very personal—the feeling is with you forever. You can't sell, donate, recycle, give it away, open a museum, or send it to space on the next charter. It's tattooed in your mind for life, even if you decide to move.

At a private club, you may confuse mouthwash with hand soap in the bathroom or find no hand soap in the bathroom of a cellar calling itself a bar. You can feel equally bored in both or have comedy blue balls about what only you can see, also in both venues. You're guaranteed to find yourself in the middle of an unbelievable story. Sure, there are other awesome cities in the world, big or small, that provide all kinds of awesome craziness. But you love what you love, don't you? Love is blind indeed.

New York changes like the live organism that it is and regardless of anything it's still good, still special. Here you meet people on trains, at shows, waiting for appointments. You see a bit of life.

Life in New York City is not about what you know,

it's about who you know. And if you're lucky—you meet wonderful people who become your friends or people to keep you company or people meant to be met for something yet undefined.

In New York, you get two minutes of quiet calm while on the subway escalator. Hudson Valley provides constant calmness, where time goes slower and nothing happens. I am lucky to have both of the worlds within a quick drive. That's right, I am very lucky with that, with people and in life in general. In fact I am so lucky that it makes most people uncomfortable.

ANALYZE THIS, ANALYZE THAT

Having rolled down the mountain,
A stone lay in the valley –
How did it fall? No one knows currently –
Did it slip from the top on its own,
Or was by someone else's will overthrown...

Aeons have flowed by,
Yet no one knows the reason why...

© Fyodor Tyutchev "Probléme"

On the map, Manhattan looks like a used condom.
Maybe that is why there're so many dicks on the island. My office is across the street from the Bureaucratic Obstacles Center, hidden among the buildings that host representatives of the International Summit of Lies and Power. Henry Miller wrote: "Forty-second Street! The top of the world, they call it. Where's the bottom then?" Oh, Mister Miller, you don't want to know. Each year, from Summit to Summit, the world lives in chaos only to confirm at the Summit that nothing can be solved, but they always express concerns. The Bureaucratic Obstacles Center might as

well be renamed into Concerns Center. Useless slackers, moving from one forum to another forum, from one buffet to another banquet, from one budget to another budget. The Bureaucratic Obstacles Center— the place for countries' representatives to meet up, eat well, and tell one another something. What is paid for must be swallowed. They've traded prestige for bank accounts and mansions. Literally, the most corrupt institution in the world. They just call it lobbying. They are so good at stealing that they need to sell merch: Corr ption t-shirt without U, because they've stolen it.

A typical, regular man is lazy. Make a man addicted to anything and he'll become committed as never before, he will make sure he does what needs to be done, he will come up with stories you've never heard heretofore, he will get up and do it no matter what. Money is very addictive. And we all have heard quite a few interesting fictional stories at the Summit.

We work with all of them to vote for or to ban something or to reflect an opinion or to point fingers. Pointing fingers at other countries can be a way to ignore the serious problems of your own. But shush.

It's funny and, at the same time, sad how big the Center is and how little they can do. Within five days of the Summit, our consulting firm is able to achieve more than the representatives do within a year. Which year? Good question.

At the Summit, the same five cocktails, all based on liquor, are served—predictability is important. The remaining ten cocktails out of a traditional total of fifteen change each year to mix things up.

China
I Am So Good I Should Start A Podcast
Vodka, Ginger Syrup, Blueberry, Lime

France
*If You Were Words On A Page, You'd Be Fine
Print*
Vodka, Tomato Juice, Lemon Juice, Worcester-
shire Sauce, Hot Sauce, Horseradish, Celery Salt,
Black Pepper

Russia
You got it? Crystal Clear!
Vodka, Birch Juice, Lime

United States
*I'm The Best There Is. I Wake Up In The Morning
And I Piss Excellence*
Vodka, Grapefruit Liqueur, Strawberry, Cucumber,
Mint, Lime

United Kingdom
I'll Have What She's Having
Vodka, Prosecco, Raspberry, Aloe Juice, Lime

Poland
*My Love For You Is Like Diarrhea. I Just Can't
Hold It In*
Whiskey, Cherry, Chocolate Bitters, Lemon

Brazil
Don't Cry Over Spilled Milk
Rum, Coffee Liqueur, Cold Pressed Coffee

Argentina
Time Heals All Wounds, Reputation, And Loans From The IMF
Tequila, Cocchi di Torino Vermouth, Amaro Montenegro, Angostura Bitters

Mozambique, Gabon, Niger
Flavored Spritzers
Pineapple, Mango, Peach

Turkey
Best Of Both Worlds Will Blow You Away
Gin, Tursu Suyu, Simple Syrup

Germany
Exercise=Endorphins. Endorphins Make People Happy. Happy People Don't Shoot Their Leg
Tequila, Cassis Liqueur, Pineapple, Lime, Orange Bitters

Japan
Brief Commercial-like Breaks Of Happiness
Mezcal, Tequila, Orgeat, Pineapple, Mint, Ginger, Lime

United Arab Emirates
Do Not Disturb
Sparkling Water

This year all countries sent their representatives to the Summit. I would also send my representative, but everyone is busy at work.

My team is so diverse it's hilarious.

Paul Triggs—international law pro who looks like a Cosa Nostra ambassador. Always polished, always with lots of gel in his black hair, always in a three-piece suit. It's like he's a completely different Paul than the one I once knew: Paul with his shirt wrinkled in the back because he sat a lot, buried in documents and files—that Paul is gone. The new Paul handles intergovernmental conflicts, international arbitration, and counseling on weird situations that got political but weren't necessarily supposed to. The new Paul also likes to be called Triggs. There's this lawyer witticism that you need to keep a suit in the office because you never know when you might be called to court. Triggs needs to keep a tuxedo in the office because he never knows when he might be called to a surprise gala or premiere.

Renat Novak—senior captain at threat management. Tech guru by day, not that by night. It wasn't me who found him. A long time ago, it was Triggs who brought him. Before going international, Triggs was a criminal defense lawyer, representing Novak in court in a very shady and complicated case, and won it.

Ian Michaud—ex-homeless ex-junkie who's an economics genius. It is surprising how much an out-patient treatment can change the skin tone of a face and overall looks. I gave him a purpose in life again, and he let himself take the needed help.

And a psychic—Lada Lembas, our networking

master who can sell anything to anyone, including the media. In hard times, people turn to drugs or religions or psychics. We've got our own taro queen. Besides, she created an annual calendar of all important world events and who's who there and who decides what. Very convenient.

To make it even more diverse we'd only need a dwarfy pony transexual that whistles and blows.

My strategic analytics department decides what the world will think about anything Russian tomorrow. No wonder they say that ideology is false knowledge. Although, to function properly a nation needs ideology. Once the crisis of ideas starts—destructions start. If a person believes in an idea, the idea becomes the driver of their life. If you want to ruin an idea—form a work group. Perhaps that will not change the world, but it will change you.

One of the test versions of obedience is an obligatory cover letter along with a resume. My rebels stood out right away: Cover letter? Here's my resume twice! There's only one method worse than that: a one-way recorded video interview with a potential employer. People are willing to do a lot of dumb things for promised future money. But my guys are the kind of people who would respond to that with a classical profanity statement, whispering into the screen.

My team itself showcases balance: balance of power, ideas, and approaches. Lada is the voice of morality whereas Ian is absolutely nuts when it comes to achieving a goal—he will chew up and spit out anyone on his way without a doubt. Triggs is a hundred percent pro laws and regulations, created by others or himself, whereas Novak can easily break a rule if he thinks that way of achieving a result is better and faster, and made-up bureaucracy blocks it. A so-called con artist in IT with principles. All together it's two sides of a coin that always forces to make a choice: follow heart or follow agenda, fairness or rules? Two verses two. And I'm the one to make the final choice. They pretty much balance out each other which puts me in the most impossible position: having to choose one of the two options—the impossible choice. It's okay: no one said it was going to be easy.

On the last day of the Summit, my team comes into my office. People have questions; they are hired to do what's needed but they also have critical thinking, which is exactly why they were hired in the first place.

"We gotta do what we gotta do, right?"

"I guess."

"For sure."

"Most likely."

"Highly likely."

"Yeah, right,"

"Fuck you, guys! It's total nonsense!"

"Hell yeah!"

"Indeed it is."

"Totally inappropriate."

"Let's change that!"

"Let's show them who's mama."

"Pssst. Let's stick to the plan."

"What's the plan?"

"What's the outcome?"

"What's the point..."

"Mirra! Say something!"

What can I say? Power has completely taken away the feeling of fear from some people if a task like "Destroy Russia" comes in from above. To have in the head two theses at the same time "America will win Russia" and "America is not a threat to Russia" is schizophrenic. However, the thesis "everyone is treated equally, understood, barbarians?" or ending a speech with the words "Alerta antifascista" and Sieg Heil salute in the end quite exist in some heads, too.

I'm at the crossroads of decisions: what to choose and which way to go. Choosing between the two options—is that really a choice? The truth is born in conversations. It might seem like too much blah blah but it's words that predefine actions.

"Let's do the mild version of ludicrous media srach for starters..." I say.

"Srach?" Ian asks. He's new.

"It means smear—acceleration of news in the media to the point of ridiculousness," Lada explains. "I'm on it!"

"What are you suggesting?" Triggs asks. "You have something on your mind, I know it, otherwise it wouldn't be you."

"Guys, we all agree that "destroying Russia" agenda is crazy and it shouldn't be happening at all, under any circumstances, don't we?" I ask my team.

They nod.

"Mirra, you didn't have to ask. Everybody understands the action-reaction concept," Novak says. "Am I right, Triggers?" Novak always comes up with new funny nicknames for Triggs; it's cute.

"Y'all, let me remind you of the existence of the Espionage Act, just in case," Triggs says.

"The ominous plan has nothing to do with it," I respond.

"Let me remind you of the U.S. Code Title 18 Chapter 113B—Terrorism," Triggs says.

"*Spaghetti Associates LLP* is right," Novak points at Triggs.

"We all are law-obedient people," I say.

"It's my job to remind." Triggs looks at Novak.

"We will be doing something very bad that may turn into something very good and fair," I say.

"So, what do you know?" Lada asks.

"What is the plan?" Novak asks.

"Ian, fill everyone in about the buckwheat plan."

"We could, to the best of our ability, mess up with the world market of buckwheat and that may or may not be the solution to what our management wants."

"May or may not?" Lada says.

"There are only a few buckwheat players in the world and Russia is one of the biggest ones," Ian says.

"That's right. Russia, the sheiks, and the subsidiaries of the United States," Triggs says.

"Maybe we should think the plan through and be sure before implementing anything?" Novak adds.

"We are sure: it's fifty-fifty. We will be doing our job anyway, cause *USA, USA*," I quietly yell the cheerleading slogan. "Our first preemptive move—the media. It spreads propaganda anyway, so let's use the news vortex for reasonable benefits."

"How? Lie about the sheiks?" Lada asks.

"Sheiks and Russia. Baloney LGBTQ+ rights in the

Middle East and, I don't know, something in Russia respectively," I say.

"Climate change fault?" Lada suggests.

"Sure. Why not? Blame them for the snow. The sheiks have to lower the production to create a shortage. Plus, make other countries stop using Russian buckwheat through their pipelines," I say.

"With other countries, it won't be for good. The United States can only supply a limited amount of liquefied buckwheat. Like Ian said, the biggest buckwheat players in the world are still the same. And the market for buckwheat is essentially the same so no other country can replace Russia," Novak says.

"The shortage can spike the demand and the price. Chances that it will are pretty high. And that may work for the benefit of Russia," Ian says.

High chance that it will? That's the hope, darling, that's the hope.

"Maybe we can do something else?" Triggs says.

"Maybe not do anything at all?" Ian suggests.

"We can't not do anything," Lada says.

"Gotta preserve balance so everyone wins," I say.

"Except other countries," Novak grins.

"Or else what, actually destroy Russia? Just for the hell of it? That's not fair." I say.

"Media srach to the rescue," Lada says and sighs.

And the team gets to the execution of the plan.

A lucky random chance would be a great life-changing solution. Randomness is a combination of facts we don't know about. Ironically, it is very American to wait for a lucky chance.

At about four o'clock in the afternoon, I enter the

World Bar across the street from the Bureaucratic Obstacles Center—the best place to think about world matters. They store my favorite sea buckthorn tea because I'm a regular here, and alcohol or soda is not my thing.

Usually, it amuses me that there are more agents in the World Bar than escorts at five-star hotels and diplomats behave worse than escorts, and, at times, they are the same people as a three-in-one combo-bombo.

The bar is surprisingly empty even though the happy hour has already started. All I hear is the sound of my shoes clattering on the floor as if beating the rhythm of my thoughts.

I always thought it would make more sense to turn the bar counter in the opposite direction, one hundred and eighty degrees, so you look not at the wall but watch people at the tables.

There are two vacant seats right near the window, and I occupy both: one for myself and one for my thoughts. At the other side of the counter is a handsome man in a suit watching the news on TV on the wall. He is Russian. I always see my people.

The bartender makes my sea buckthorn tea with a little bit of mint, chilled, and served in a foggy glass. Mint, it turns out, works wonders, and a few cups of tea make it easy and almost not offensive that the world might go to shit in nuclear weapons threat.

I don't necessarily believe in destiny, but some things are meant to happen regardless of anyone's volition. The man orders Miraval rosé, my favorite wine from the past that changes the present; it exudes aromas of fresh fruit, currants, and fresh rose with a zest of lemon.

"According to the doctrine on the use of nuclear weapons, the Russian Federation will not use them preventively," the Russian man says in Russian language with a distinctive Moscow accent, mostly to himself, commenting on the TV news.

"Pumping up the media space," I say to him. "Or they raise the stakes for something."

"For what?"

"I don't know yet. We all will find out soon on the same TV channel," I reply.

He nods. I sip my tea.

"This is not the best way to annoy Russia if they really want to," I say.

"And what would that be?" the Russian man looks at me.

"I try not to speak publicly about politics."

"Is that so?"

"It divides the world into friends and foes. And all people are friends by default."

"There are strangers."

"There are no strangers—just people we haven't met."

Alcohol is a lubricant of human relations, they say. Well, not necessarily. In the United States, you are automatically friends based on your native language. Pal Petrovich speaks Russian and that fact automatically makes him my friend because I speak Russian too. And it's just one of those situations when you say what you think without thinking about repercussions as it should be with true freedom of speech. Besides, who would dare say anything at all while agents are listening? No one! That means the information shared publicly is no secret.

"Okay, fine. I'll tell you what I think,"

"Do tell," Pal Petrovich says and smiles.

"The best way to annoy anyone, especially Russia, would be mass gaslight when propaganda pipeline pumps the news about anything but truth." I give an inkling.

"Where are the hidden interests?"

"Reputation damage. That can't be fixed short term. Or a banal way to annoy—economic damage, like blocking the buckwheat price," I say.

"When I was a kid, I had severely crossed eyes," Pal Petrovich says. "One looked outside and up, an-other—inside and down. It was impossible to tell where I was looking, ever. My eyes looked in one di-rection, and people thought I looked in the other di-rection and acted accordingly. Often, I tried to explain to them that I didn't do it on purpose and what it all meant. Asking for petty is never a winning position. It wasn't easy for me either until I got surgery to fix it. Or so I thought," Pal Petrovich says.

"Do you think opponents don't see or don't want to see the change even after the surgery?" I ask. "They still don't get the essence?"

"The truth is somewhere in between," he says.

"And we might actually not know what's going on at all," I provoke and wait for the answer that doesn't keep me waiting long.

"Oh, Mirra, we know," he says and finishes his wine. "Not all, but we know some."

And if we don't, we act like we know anyway.

"I'll see you around, Mirra." Pal Petrovich pays his check.

"I have to go, too. Have a good one."

And it happens so that unintentionally, one by one, we leave the World Bar, walk towards the same parking next to it, and stand one next to another while our cars are driven out of their parking lots to the exit.

"Holy molly! Moskvich? Really? I haven't seen this car since visiting my grandparents for summer vacation as a kid. Although, my grandfather's Moskvich was blue," Pal Petrovich exclaims.

Yeah, I know, my car is a head-turner. Initially, I wanted to buy something cool and unusual, like Staten Island ferry or similar, and ended up with an orange Moskvich made in nineteen eighty-one. Besides, living in the Hudson Valley, I need a car. Mine is a supermodel in a homeless coat. I gave it a nickname: Absurd.

"Is it all redone?" Pal Petrovich asks, walking around it like a kid with a toy.

"On the inside, this Moskvich is mostly made of German parts, the seats are Italian, the tech and outside is restored original." I am very proud of my car.

"Wow! I am impressed and surprised. Your car doesn't look what it is on the inside at all," Pal Petrovich says.

"That is the whole point," I wink. And I leave.

Regardless of the world events, private life goes on and it's important to dedicate time to keep friendships alive and family happy.

On September twenty-ninth, I incorporated Apricot Jam Day—a holiday, the annual get-together for a closed circle to summarize our yearly events; it happens to be right after the International Summit of Lies and Power. Also, not everything needs a reason.

Each year, friends gather at my house for dinner and a special dessert by my family's recipe: apricot jam, my favorite deliciousness that's meant to be shared. I cut apricots in half, take out the seed and those two meaty halves float in apricot syrup in a glass jar for a few months before Jam Day. It is exactly the way I remember it from my childhood.

My friend of ten years, Frank Ellis, left my life without any particular reason. Right before he disappeared, we had one of our usual conversations about everything and nothing, and touched on the world politics topic; Russia and the United States specifically. Let's face it—it's always those parts of the globe, always those civilizations; not Australia versus Canada or Iceland versus Dominican Republic.

I guess Frank didn't like my frank opinion and thought he was the only one allowed to be frank. I accepted his different opinion. He deprived me of the opportunity to have an opinion at all. Modern democracy as is—one opinion and the wrong one. So Frank self-isolated by his own volition. Oh, well. It's for the better. I did not want to check whether it was a friendly tight hug or friendly asphyxia. Friends who turn out to be not friends are like a virus that's not visual. I've reached zen and started to acknowledge things philosophically: some people help with their presence, some help with their absence. I don't hate Frank. Hate is a very strong feeling, like love—you have to earn it.

There's always balance in life. You lose something only to gain something. The movement goes on. Like a soda can that's rolling downhill—downhill, but moving. Like money that also needs movement—you've got to spend it to have more of it. I know, the logic is not logical but otherwise, there's no room in the metaphorical pockets for circulation. Movement is life.

That way I gained a lit agent that became my manager. Elana Dor Agency: opening doors and managing talent worldwide. Elana dug out two of my self-published novels and sold them to the big publisher. There were talks about the movie, but then Elana found out the story didn't consist of a prequel and a sequel, but had five separate storylines with the same protagonist, all already written, all already self-published a while back. So she decided to turn the book series into a hit and do a miniseries show of five episodes, ninety minutes each—"Empire Building Says Hi." Natasha Lyonne would be perfect for the role, and Elana is doing her best to sell it to a streaming service.

My manager Elana Dor, "beautiful orchid", a forty-five-year-old redhead who looks like a female version of Einstein. She is the only person I accept writing criticism from, and my stubbornness and unwillingness to change the text much pays off for both of us. They say the industry is very subjective. I agree and do it my way. I'm the artist—I see it that way. Shut up and buy my books.

The Universe sometimes gives you what you want

but with a question mark. When I couldn't afford to write full-time, my work didn't bring satisfaction. Now, I can afford to write full-time, and my work brings so much satisfaction I don't want to leave it. And what to choose?

I know I can get pretty much anything I want. It's only a matter of time for wishes to come true.

I wanted a timeless cool-kids-club for those who appreciate creatives and laid-back, affordable luxury—I got Awesome Month: hotel, retreat, and social club all in one. It's in Big Sur where one decompresses from content, goes for a walk, enjoys yourself, does nothing. There's so much nothing you can do. Serenity. The only purpose of Awesome Month is to enjoy life, all month long, month by month, every month. I got the land, and Dylan's investment firm took care of the rest. They believed in the idea more than I did and gave it the magic kick.

I wanted a ginger cat—I started looking for a ginger cat and became a conspiracy theorist, accidentally, not on purpose. As it turned out adopting a kitten in New York City is close to impossible. They want you to fill out numerous applications with the stupidest question "In case you die, what's going to happen to the pet?" *Bitch, I don't know! I haven't thought about it regarding to my children yet!*

Maybe they never actually wanted to let a pet go because they'd be out of pets, and pets mean donations. Maybe a specific pet breed was a cover for a drug type, and there I was with numerous questions about the pet's character and health. Of course, they got annoyed. And maybe that is why they made it ridiculously hard to adopt, coming up with all sorts of rejections.

> You don't have a private circus in the back-yard. Goodbye.

> We only let people named Rachel adopt. Sor-ry, not sorry, not Rachel.

> It's Thursday and your recommendation letter person is not an engineer from Iowa, so no-no.

Some cats and dogs are allergic to people. At that point, I hated all people and still needed people, be-cause without people I wouldn't be able to hate peo-ple.

Petfinder was more like Petgrinder—they cut your mind into mulch until you gave up and bought the pet you wanted instead. That is what I did: a happy cat without a traumatic history—ginger Tabby Martishka. And a dog, of the happy breed as well—red Poodle Mimosa.

What else has happened in the past two years? My friends Mason Reeve and Nora Sparks were together until they were not. Love is life. That's how you know you're alive. Work and hobbies can bring satisfaction until they become a routine. Can love become a rou-tine? And if it does, what happens then? Oh...right...

I knew it was going to end, probably before they did. One day, out of nowhere, Mason booked a long weekend trip to Antigua and went there for a vaca-tion, alone, so he said. He then sent me pictures saying how he was enjoying his time alone. In one of the pictures, Mason's sunglasses had a reflection of a woman in a white miniskirt. Due to his profession, Mason is secretive. I knew this. I didn't ask him questions he couldn't answer. That was not the case. There's a difference between couldn't and wouldn't. So, he was being secretive for personal reasons. Mason messed up, and he knew I knew. The best you can do for people is let them be in charge of their own decisions. I didn't say anything to Nora—what's between the two of them is none of my business. But the two are also my friends so they had to figure this out. And soon thereafter they did—they broke up, until one night that led to one very cute baby and one even more dramatic break up again.

Nora is out because she distanced herself from me and everyone else for whatever reason. Maybe one day she'll come back, I don't know. All I know is that she became a fan of piercing, which Mason describes as her having bullets coming out of her face and body. Well, that's it.

And Mason bought a teal motorcycle and a box full of batteries of various kinds and sizes. "So I'll never have to buy batteries again—they'll last me a lifetime," he said. Well, that is also a way to manage a crisis.

Dylan and I, on the contrary, have been having so much fun like never before. He's been around for so long that I gave him a nickname, and then I gave him another nickname—that's how long I've known him. Our inner jokes, not meant for anyone to understand, are amazing.

My boobs look like a twelve-year-old's, so I call

them my twelve-year-old girls.

"They stopped growing at twelve," I once said.

"The same thing happened to my dick," Dylan tittered.

"Do note it wasn't me who said it," I giggled.

But we both thought it. We surely have a lot in common—a sense of humor. And we are indeed a match: he has Crocks, I have Uggs—evenly ugly footwear to maintain true romance.

He got me a two-carat ring called *Edge*. It looks very badass and fits my personality very well. I got him a neon sward, which, I know for sure, he uses in our closet to fight the imaginary enemy.

Also, Dylan put on some weight. His guilty pleasure is hotdogs. I have no idea why. Dylan guzzles hot dogs as if inside they had classified documents that had to be destroyed immediately. As a result, he looks like an Omnomnivore and Borat neighbor's wife combined. One time, I told him he should eat healthy—he got hysterical and made a scene. Another time he wanted to eat shit—I encouraged him to have more fast food to get his cholesterol level to the maximum so he'd have a heart attack faster, and I'd finally live happily ever after. Whereupon, he chose chicken, hummus, and vegetables for dinner. Men...

This year's Apricot Jam Day is very hot—thanks, global warming. With this tendency, soon enough, people will migrate to Siberia and Arctics just for some breeze and fresh air.

Our menu is always based on the nationality of everyone present at dinner. The only exception is I serve food, not cuisine. Food is supposed to make you feel full and happy and not sit pretentiously at the table with four different forks talking about modern art that nobody understands. This year, we have Russian, American, Italian, and Middle Eastern.

And, of course, apricot jam—the star of this day.

And pickled watermelons—my favorites. Dylan says I kill the freshness of a fruit. I say that by pickling, I preserve it, like Lenin's body in the Kremlin.

And homemade soft drink Kvas. Dylan wants to start the manufacture and sell Kvas to Whole Foods. He is professionally damaged, seeing a startup in just anything; next—building a kvas pipeline worldwide.

Apricot jam and pickled watermelons. Sugar and salt. Sweet and sour. One way or the other. The infinite choice.

"Oh my god, it smells good," Elana says.

"Did you know people can smell different stuff in each nostril?" Dylan says.

"Smelling stereo Dolby surround? Nice," Mason says as we all take our seats.

"Ate all your hotdogs today yet?" I ask Dylan.

"Mirra..."

"I know how you can combine all possible forms of dopamine at once: eat hotdogs and jerk off to a stand-up special." It'd be easier for him to agree with me than listen to my irksome comments—I need him to stop eating crap food for good.

"Stop treating my body like it's Tamagotchi!" Dylan flips.

"If I stop, this Tamagotchi," I point at Dylan, "without all the arbitrary things it will just start to moan, malfunction, and will die, and I'll have to start all over again with the new Tamagotchi. And let me tell you this: while I'm alive, you will live and suffer! From good nutrition, exercise, and willpower."

"That is the sweetest thing anyone ever said to me," Dylan breaks into a smile and smooches me.

"Shut up and eat your broccoli."

"Broccoli can suck my dick," Dylan mumbles.

"I don't think technology has come that far," I say.

"What if it's a life or death situation that you need to eat bacon to survive?" Dylan says.

"It's hard to imagine that very high pathetical situation, but if a chicken can purr and bacon can save a life, then fine—you can have it," I say.

"Mirra, have you been recruited by any special force?" Mason asks.

"Why?" I ask.

"Because you interrogate me like a sleuth, that's why," Dylan says.

"Right after college, I was recruited by the special agency in Ukraine. They wanted me to write for the news agency. All agents can't go abroad because of the secrecy level they hold. National security doesn't want them to leave the country and start trading secrets. They also don't make any decent money for the very stressful work that they do. The only thing they can actually afford is a one-way plane ticket and hope for the best they can trade the secrets they know."

"Is that how you came to the US?" Dylan laughs.

"Yes, that is exactly what happened," I reply.

"So, did you work for them?" Mason asks.

"Volunteer for propaganda?! No, thanks. I declined. Besides, once in the system—always in the system. No thanks again."

As we have dinner, I suggest playing the game "I don't understand". The beauty of this game is that it lets you speak your mind without being considered rude or politically incorrect; it lets you express what you really think about anything. This way you can get to know one another, making the small talk interesting. And the game is basically complaining about minor random things, which always brings New Yorkers together. And New York runs on coffee, booze, and complaints.

"I was trained to go into danger first, so I'll start," Mason says. "I don't understand when people proclaim: 'Oh, I'm Italian' and the only family member from Italy is their second cousin of their great grandmother's new boyfriend's aunt." Mason is a hundred percent Italian.

"What about those who are fifty-fifty: half one nationality, half the other?" I ask.

"Depends on identification. Make a choice and stick to it," Mason replies.

"I identify as Wild Empress after three glasses of wine," Elana says.

"The world I want to live in is wild empresses not spilling drinks on pool tables," Mason says.

"You just haven't played pool with me, hun," Elana winks.

"Don't!" I yell and look at both Mason and Elana. "My manager is only mine. My FBI guy is only mine. Don't even! I can't lose more friends." I imply Nora.

"Hahaha, okay. Take it easy," Mason says.

"The world I want to live in is folks not using white

towels to wipe off all their makeup." Elana wisely changes the subject. "I don't understand why anyone would ignore water."

"Maybe that's a new Instagram technique to spread their makeup all over the face, mixing foundation and mascara and lipstick all in one like contemporary art," I say.

"You can look at someone's Instagram on your computer without having an account for about ten seconds, and then it gets locked. That is exactly the healthy amount of time spent on someone's 'happy' life. After that, it becomes nerve-racking and whether you want it or not, you start comparing your life to what you see and filters always win," Dylan says.

"I once spent about twenty minutes on Instagram watching pimples being squeezed out. And you know the worst part? The sensations while watching those clips were the same as popping bubble wrap!" I say.

"Oh, those are the worst guilty pleasures! So satisfying—it's insane," Elana reacts.

"I've never had any social media outside of occasional temporary dating apps," Mason says.

"I can't believe that neither of us here uses social media yet we still talk about it and know all about it," I say.

"We're very social people," Dylans says.

"YouTube is no different. It wants you to never close it. You can also turn on a video, leave the room for twenty-five minutes, come back and some dumb commercial will still be on. When did they start making commercials this long? I don't get it," Elana says.

"And it's always a first-person review advertising

some cream or blush or socks or online therapy or other nonsense," Dylan says.

"YouTube is where I find out new made-up words like facialist or mixologist," Mason says.

"I'm a mixologist every time I make crepes, mixing flour and milk and water and stuff," I say.

"Who's a mixologist?" Dylan says.

"A bartender in a New York City bar that is trying too hard," Mason says.

"If I ever mix-up someone's birthday I'll say I'm a mixologist," Dylan says.

"Every man is a mixologist then," Elana says.

"Okay, my turn," Dylan says. "There's a national disaster with emotions in this country and I don't understand why it happened and what exactly caused it. Everybody wants you to care how they feel but no one can bear an actual emotion; there's a pill to not feel an emotion, there's a pill to feel an emotion recreating genuine and natural emotions—only the good ones. No one wants to feel bad ever, not even for a minute."

"A very banal statement yet accurate: can't appreciate the good without the bad. Avoidance of the bad is a disservice to yourself, swiping the dust under the carpet. A person can deceive themself, but not fate," I say. "What I don't understand is why I'm not the world-famous writer yet, Elana?" and I wink.

"I'm working on it and you're kind of already halfway there," Elana says.

"Oh, she has news," Dylan says.

"Two, actually. I wanted to keep them for dessert but since you asked: Switzerland is obsessed with your writing, Mirra. The bankers and businessmen want a good laugh. Your sense of humor is very masculine. Eighty-four percent of your audience is men."

"Have they seen my picture?" I ask.

"No. You don't show any!" Elana says.

"That is how you know they like the jokes indeed. Okay, Dylan, you can say it." I look at Dylan.

"See? I told you so. It's happening," Dylan says.

"I am also selling you to China," Elana says.

"You taking away my passport now or I can say goodbye to my loved ones before this slavery?"

"So silly, Mirra. I'm selling the rights to China."

"Am I going on a tour?" I ask.

"Yes," Elana says.

"Ugh, but I don't want to."

"Ugh, but you have to."

"Just take twenty percent for international rights and let's not go anywhere," I suggest.

"Oh, you're going. And then I'll sell a show of grandma Mirra complaining all the time," Elana says.

"I'd watch a show like that. You don't complain at all," Dylan says to Elana.

"I can't complain. I mean I can, but the world won't change if I do," Elana says.

"Imagine you complain and that immediately changes. That could be an awesome superpower," Mason says.

"No need. China and Switzerland pretty much cover all book sales you want, and I want," Elana says to me.

"Well, now I want more!" I say.

"Never enough..." Mason says.

After dinner, as I prepare the set up for apricot jam

and tea, going back and forth between the house kitchen and the dinner table outside near the fire pit, I look at the scene and think: who cares about self-realization, career, money anymore? *This* is already awesome! Sometimes I dream about having a simple country lifestyle: pickle watermelons and sauerkraut with cranberries, plant flowers and water them with a sprinkler hose, raise children and care for my pets, read philosophy books and write satire. On some level, it scares me that it might come true because wishes do come true.

When I bring out the mugs for tea, I can't help but overhear Elana and Dylan talking at the table.

"...although this popsicle is technically naked..." Dylan says.

"Use protection," Elana says.

"Nah, I like to live dangerously with my frozen treats. I'm imagining little baby popsicles running around," Dylan says.

I am pretty sure I don't want to know the context and details of that conversation so I sit next to Mason near the fire pit.

"Am I hallucinating or they are talking about popsicles having babies?" Mason asks with surprise on his face.

"I'm gonna excuse myself from the popsicle topic." I smile.

"How is everything with you?" Mason says.

"Quite boring. Russia is the evil on the agenda again. No variety whatsoever," I reply. "What's new with you?"

"I bought a dreamcatcher."

"Mason, what are you trying to catch? Not enough of catching running around the world?" I say.

"Just trying to catch something good for a change —a good dream will suffice," Mason says. He suffers from sleep disorders.

"For a good night's sleep hang the dreamcatcher, get into bed, undercovers...or is it too many under-covers for you?" I say.

He smiles.

"You just made my day better because I got bad news," Mason says.

"What bad news?" I get serious.

"A voluntold deployment I can't get out of. It's very bad. It's at the Mexican border," Mason says.

"Best tacos ever!" I say.

"Certainly not worth it," Mason says.

"Can Nora give you a doctor's note of some sort that is good enough to avoid deployment but continue regular work duties?" I ask.

"Nora declined. She's angry at me," Mason says.

"What for?" I say.

"For not willing to marry a lier when she tricked me into her pregnancy," Mason says and his vein on the neck starts pulsating.

"Mason, common. It's not like you didn't know how babies are made," I say.

"She said she was on a pill and couldn't get preg-nant. She's a doctor and knows her body better."

"That's what she said?" I start laughing.

"I know, I know," Mason facepalms. "Sleeping with an ex is bad luck. One time—one mistake."

"You two have a child and you're still arguing

about who's right and wrong?" I say.

Mason looks dejected as if I'm scolding him like a little child and sighs: "Mirra, out of all people you understand pain. I was tormented by the fact that I wasn't tormented. Deep down she's a good person. I don't want her to suffer. I just want her to see that I don't suffer anymore. And she doesn't let me live my life."

"Do you? Do you let yourself live your life?" I say. "Look, I was hurt before too and used to hide my feelings deep inside because I was afraid of being hurt again. That's a way of living for sure. It's not bad, but it's also not good. But you know what? It's already been half of life, literally. And what if the only way to feel alive again is to be vulnerable? To let yourself be vulnerable? Don't you ever miss being loved?"

"It's complicated." Mason sighs again.

"Whatever it is that she wants you to do and promised to ruin your career if you don't, through blackmail or whatever... Maybe buy your balls back from the pawn shop and stop being afraid. Mason, time flies, love goes away—not so complicated."

When you have an alternative—you feel good. But what should you do if one day you need an alternative for the alternative?

OPINION SHAKER

Orange—the color of happiness. My socks match the color of my vintage car with no tech in it. Let's see if a mirrored response can be matched on another level with tech.

Washington, D.C., is like a giant office city. And it smells of something bitter, like all alien cities smell. My orange Moskvich is the brightest spot in this gloomy city. I drive my Absurd in the parking garage of the Star Democracy Freedom Group headquarters, looking tired: I guess I am assimilating with this gloomy office city—the quagmire on the hill.

First, it was walking with a Walkman, then with a portable disk player, then iPod, then phone—always with music, imagining things, saving myself from reality. I've been walking a lot. Now I keep my music in my car and things are very goddamned real.

The office is a large space with typical cubicles, grey walls, low ceilings, and square white lamps imitating daylight. Only select individuals have access to the window—they've suffered enough to get to the natural light. I can't...the office... Jobs with sun access should be the highest paid. The closer to the sun—the more privileged you are. Office plankton should be at the bottom of the salary spectrum and street sweepers at the top.

Only now it makes sense why in Hollywood movies there's always a guy who brings a rifle to his office and shoots everyone, at least in his thoughts for sure. Funny enough, some Hollywood movies are produced with a specific agenda in mind curated exactly by offices like that, which makes them almost documentary and factually accurate.

While walking towards the door of Lars Fiting, I see lots of different posters on the walls, some of them hung askew.

*Any employees who wish to participate in a group photo, please meet us in the vestibule between the glass and wooden doors today at 2:30 pm for Purple Thursday

October is Domestic Violence Awareness Month (DAM). Domestic violence continues to be a profound and pervasive social and public health crisis, crossing lines of class, race, ethnicity, and sexuality. Join us for Purple Thursday by wearing purple to raise awareness and show our support for those who experience domestic violence and abuse and to let them know that help is available for them and their families.
To participate in supporting Purple Thursday, we encourage all to please share a

group photo of staff wearing purple. We thank you all for your support.

The domestic violence statistics, while not the worst in the world, are on the high end. The United States is the only industrialized nation that has failed to ratify the convention of Bureaucratic Obstacles Center on eliminating discrimination against women, which specifically refers to violence against women as a form of discrimination. Just saying.

Damn, you DAM! I used to like the purple color a lot. Not anymore.

"THERE IS HOPE,
even when your brain tells you there isn't."

"SELF-CARE ISN'T
SELFISH.
You can't pour from an empty cup - TAKE CARE OF YOURSELF FIRST."

Did you know?
1 IN 5 ADULTS
in the U.S. experiences a mental health condition.
LESS THAN HALF
GET TREATMENT.

It's ok to not be ok.
Seeking help is a sign of help, not weakness.

Yes, in those crazy fonts. That's so depressing. Might as well use one of those posters and call the hotline. VAI! (Violence Awareness International) VAI! VAI! Help!

"Mirra! You made it," Lars greets me.

"Lars! We need to talk. Let's go eat somewhere."

"The world is in crisis, Mirra."

"Yeah, but I'm hungry. Besides, these anti-depression posters make me depressed."

"Ha. Right? They should've done just one poster: Live, laugh, toaster in your bath," Lars says.

"Let's go."

At lunch, I understand something: we judge people not because we disagree with what they do but because their behavior is inconvenient to us.

First, the server takes our order and instead of saying nothing he starts to insist I get my Calf's liver medium-rare and not well-done as I wanted. Calf's liver below well-done is disgusting. I know it for sure.

Why do men argue with me? And why do some men think they are entitled to give any advice at all?

Then, at the table close to us, senior people get their order faster than we do.

"Didn't we order before them?" Lars asks.

"They need it faster—they are way older and may not stay till the end of the meal," I say.

"First come, first serve takes on a new meaning," Lars says. "Did you do anything fun observing Columbus Day?"

"Yes. I went to the store to buy spices and got lost."

Lars titters and then says: "I'm getting married for the third time. Did you receive your invitation?"

"Nothing in the mail yet. How do you have time to get married three times?" I ask.

"Prioritizing. Sometimes instead of fucking up the world it's better to fuck a woman and see how you feel thereafter," Lars replies.

Lars Fiting is the Chief of Information Service of the Presidential Secretariat and the Head of the National Commission on Freedom of Speech and Development of the Information Industry. He has a nose for things, too. He watched me for a year. I proved to be astute. After making sure he could trust me, he actually started to trust me.

"Listen, Mirra, at some point, we will have to escalate and we're probably going to send our troops soon, so just in case—be ready to accommodate the informational frontline," Lars says.

"Are you kidding? A more inapt scenario I cannot imagine. On what ground?" I exclaim.

"Does it matter? We always find something. Democracy is in danger—that still works."

"Lars, the entire army on the balance sheet of the country is called peacekeepers, and the entire real army is a private military company. So which troops?"

"Take one guess," Lars replies. "Action intended to aggrandize America. That's the only way fair."

"Fairness? Or vengeance for their mere existence? You know you can't do that. The Marines absolutely cannot stand on that soil, or else that genius cliffhanger will provoke the nuke inferno," I say.

"Nah, forget the Marines. Estonian Mormons—our best bicycle troops. They don't drink, they don't smoke, they are like ferocious robots ready to execute orders. Brutal thugs in PMC," Lars says.

"If you proceed, irreversible processes will begin, the big change, the restructure of everything. All it takes is to respect Russia and consider it an equal. How can one yell about the importance of equality and not follow your own rules?" I say.

"Welcome to the real world of rules," Lars purses his mouth in a self-satisfied smirk. "The Congress will have to be in sync."

"The lower house, the upper house, the mad house, the trap house—all of them?" I pause and then add: "If Russia decides..."

Lars interrupts me: "Russia, decides, blah blah blah... Futile attempts of domination. They won't do anything anyway—still too weak," he jeers.

Driblets of his saliva land on my face. *Am I infected with a democracy venom now?*

"This can't be going on for long. Everybody will get tired and sooner or later, rather sooner, diplomacy needs to be applied to avoid major fatigue," I say.

"No. Russia can't win. Not even nominally, because it'll be a kick in the nuts of the ill American ego with the paramount importance," Lars says.

When is it not ill?

"It has to be on our terms. No one knows a way to stop this on our terms. So no one's stopping," Lars continues. "I'm not the only one in this: there are other people with interests and their jesters and lobbyists and ideology bigots and politicians winning points in attempts to get to the helm of this ship; one group in dissension with the other, and God knows whether they know what they're doing," Lars says.

"Lars, you don't mind giving Russia a little bit so everyone else can take a breath and take a break, do you?" I clarify.

"Like what?" Lars asks.

"What if something malefic happens, beyond our control, that turns out to be for the benefit of Russia? That technically doesn't mean that Russia wins?" I suggest. "I don't know, like a sheik decides to lower the production of buckwheat and Russia becomes the only one who can produce enough regardless of sanctions. Would that be okay?" I say.

"Subtle argument. That's too much for them."

"What other option do you have? For how long can you rely on the gay lobby against the sheiks? Not for long. The sheiks are, of course, interested in profits, choosing the economic benefits above all, but accusations in the media can make them angry and change their decision towards cooperation with Russia. The silver lining: your governors will win high points with the gay lobby. Everything will be hunky-dory," I say.

"Whence this confidence? Whose side are you on?"

Lars, you keep forgetting who I am. "Whose side are *you* on? You say you want it stopped but, at the same time, escalate. Belying, don't you think? Do all players fully understand the repercussions of each outcome, like for real? So what do you really want?"

"Honestly?" Lars sighs. "I want to marry my young soon-to-be-wife, go for a honeymoon to a sunny island, retire, and have my four-o-one deposited ASAP. Sending troops is insane, but hey, what can one do?"

"You can have your peace soon." I offer.

"Yeah, right!" Lars says sarcastically. "Good luck

making arrangements with a sheik."

"I heard you." I smile and take it for the green light.

"If you can do that, I'll owe you one," Lars says and leans back contentedly on his chair.

"Lars, can you do me a little favor? I say.

"And in return?" Lars says.

"Didn't you just say you'll owe me one?" I say.

"Did you solve the crisis yet?" Lars says.

"Fine. And in return, I'll disperse in the media that in Russia, due to sanctions, there aren't enough breast implants for transgender people, and cut-off dicks are being stolen and then sold on the black market of organs in Europe; and offended BDSM community in Europe protests against BSM (born as men) who, they claim, have stolen not just their dicks but also letters."

"Oh, Jesus Christ. Deal. What kind of favor?"

"Reverse voluntold deployment of my FBI friend. He is in good standing with the agency, he always goes everywhere he's told. This time, he shouldn't: he's got a toddler, he's going through a lot right now, and he'll get suicidal at the location of deployment. You want your best staff around. Posters in the office won't help." I say.

"What is his name?" Lars is very direct.

"Mason Reeve."

"I'll see what I can do. In the meantime you've got to deliver. They should never have a single day without pressure," Lars says.

"Transgender or Russians?" I grin.

"Whatever. Both," Lars says.

"Drag queens will drag them on Twitter," I smile.

"Mirra, don't forget the media srach," Lars says.

"Needless to repeat twice. I got it the first time."

"Good luck," Lars says.

On the Chess app, a guy texted: "Pussy! Face like a man" during our game when I was doing a trick on him.

That's right, hun. I am a pussy. Literally. But thanks for the "additional guarantee" idea.

Modern Western society can view men as being totally useless but somehow in charge of everything. Indeed. Good luck to me being a woman and making sure things happen my way in a man's world. Especially if your friend is a world-class pimp.

Time to let yourself fly, United said. Okay then, let's fly to unite.

Dubaisk is very hot and beautiful, almost like a mirage in the middle of a desert. Everyone is very bright and shiny, with a saucepan sheen—the show-off epidemic is contagious. Froufrou, froufrou.

Val Zironka stays at the best hotel because she doesn't accept anything less than the best. She's been living here for the past year or so, mostly for work. My friend Val is a high-end pimp; we call her producer.

Dubaisk is a unique place. It has so much silicon in human bodies per square meter that it's unsanitary. Here, like nowhere else in the world, no one has ever refused a freebie. A lot of untouched seafood leftovers and a flyer in Russian language "Back pain booboo? Boobira's clinic", as well as faces of people who don't look like they're ever in a hurry—something I will never forget.

In the Western world trampling your soles at the

speed of an enraged parrot equals a path to success, the faster the better. Hmm...is it though? Not everyone needs success in the form it is being sold. Not everyone wants to be a boss. Everyone wants to be happy. Happiness does not equal being a boss. Makes you think... Traveling is not valuable. The conclusions you have drawn thanks to the trip are.

At the hotel restaurant, where we are having dinner, some tables have luxury bags on them, and it's women only who sit at those tables.

"What's going on with etiquette rules in Dubaisk? Don't women know that putting a bag on the table is bad manners?" I say after we order.

"It's the price." Val shrugs.

"Price for what?" I take a nibble at bread.

"Price for the owner of the bag, Mirra. If it's Louis Vuitton—it's only about two grand. If it's Hermes—then it's a bit more expensive."

"And everyone knows about it?" I ask.

"The price is unofficial. Those who need to know—they know," Val replies.

Right to this day, I thought that nothing could surprise me in life but Jesus Christ this is unbelievable; and kind of sad that beautiful women, whose lives are priceless, have the price of a handbag.

"Val, so those are all sex workers?"

"Not necessarily. Some of them are escorts, some are looking for a better life in exchange for their beauty and obedience, and some are looking for a husband. They think that by finding a sugar daddy, they won't have to work anymore. No one tells them that being a sugar baby is way more work than at the office—more beneficial, sure, but also more exhausting and stressful."

We eat our appetizers without saying a word.

"Mirra, don't stress. As the old saying goes: all diseases are from stress and only syphilis is from pleasure," Val finally breaks the silence and laughs. "To work or not to work is only by their own volition."

"Is it though? Or is it because it's extremely hard to make a decent living in a small town where they live and Instagram daily 'attacks' with this lifestyle, projecting fake luxury..."

"Stop it!" Val interrupts me in annoyance. No one forces anyone into anything. They want a better life and this is the fastest way for the majority of these women. None of them have a pussy horizontally—it's all vertical, so neither of them is unique, like a snowflake in the blizzard of dicks. Besides, oftentimes they do get married and are happily in love with their husbands. And in case of a divorce within seven years, they get stupid rich on the way out."

"Val, I just want every pussy in this world to live so happily and steadily to be able to form a union."

"Me too! The good kind of me too," Val smirks and then adds, "Aha. Twat With Ears Union. Pay your dues on time."

"And a dead clam for a logo 'cause a shaved twat looks exactly like that." And we both start laughing.

"In all seriousness, though, girls haven't been lucky recently and seem like derelict mansions," Val says.

"Why?"

"Look at all the bags. Mirra, It's too many of them, especially this time of the year. Most governors and businessmen have been out of here since the last day of the International Summit of Lies and Power. Where did they all go? Back to work, suddenly? If they stopped fucking—something terrible is going to happen. Up until recently, it used to be very good times and everyone spent a lot of money on having fun. I called it the golden era when girls filled out a charter plane that flew them to Dubaisk for the week-end, after which they bought houses at home. And so did I. Sheiks don't carry cash with them, and anytime one liked a girl, he just took off a Rolex from his wrist and gave it to her. On the way home the plane was filled with girls with three Rolex watches on each wrist. Fun times... Eh, I have an uncanny feeling that trouble is coming," Val concludes.

"Trouble? Like what?" I ask.

"I don't know. Something big. And it might affect all of us," Val says.

Where did they all go? To save their assets. If only Val knew that the struggle was already happening and not only for material values. Flightradar must have gone crazy when they were leaving Dubaisk, because heads of large companies do not fly on the same plane for safety reasons. Val's right: it is not the craziest crazy we have seen so far.

"So, aside from work, how have you been?" I ask.

"I don't do anything toxic anymore: food, nail pol-ish, relationships. And I'm going through no brand phase, meaning no brand brings satisfaction."

"Val, that can't be it. Do tell." I insist.

"Eh... I recently went on a date with one super cute guy, who got offended with I-don't-even-know-what, called me a single middle-aged woman with a cat, and left thirty minutes into the date, yelling on his way out to go fuck myself."

"Don't tell me you took offense," I say.

"Of course not. I never understood that expression. What's wrong with go fuck yourself? Everyone does it anyway. How's that supposed to be offensive? Besides, I *am* a single middle-aged woman with a cat—those are plain facts. It's just...I feel like people are suddenly crazy and stupid at the same time. Mirra, I can't even get drunk anymore because when I do, I become too emotional for nothing."

"Oh, someone's having a crisis."

"I'm tired of everything. It's all the same, even the films are all the same, and the names of the characters are unimportant because they are not remembered, but they are also all the same. *Father of the Bride*, *First Love*, *Anatomy of a Murder*, *Robbery*, *Head to Head*. I already know how the events in each movie will develop and how they will end," Val sighs. "It's all the same: restaurants, conversations, food."

"People?" I ask.

"No. People aren't the same. I love people."

"Well, I love people too, but that's not what you want to say."

"Mirra, I just want to love one particular person, a man...I want love to happen naturally and not because I created circumstances for that..." Val says. Her face looks lugubrious. "I want us to grow together as personalities and make the world a better place, and what do I see on a man's dating profile? 'I can teach you how to whistle and will happily peel your orange'."

"Yeah, that's a really low bar," I say. "Dating apps are weird. They erase the beauty of the unknown and eradicate the effort: the two powers that make us move forward."

"Mirra, we're living in a fucked up world now. Everyone is so afraid that a woman is wrongfully objectified that women nowadays are like: Hello! Can anyone please objectify me just a little bit? Please? Because you know what? Soon enough when face skin withers and buttocks sags, I won't be able to be objectified at all!" Val says.

"If only there was such thing as free dinners at dates. A good meal is expensive, but energy is priceless," I say.

"At times, I'd rather choose popcorn for dinner at home than a questionable company," Val says.

Independence is one empty place. Planes don't fly there, trains don't go there, cars don't drive there. It's the vacuum. Even to use a vacuum cleaner, you need a mess to begin with. And only another person, a meaningful person, can help you create a mess so the place is no longer empty. Loneliness is the pandemic of our high-tech time.

"Val, how can I help?"

"You're already doing it—listening to my crisis of meaning or age or whatever the hell I have. Thanks."

A woman has all kinds of thanks.

Thanks—a typical white girl squeaks out the word with disgust.

Thanks—"Ugh, good luck"

Thanks—a diplomatic "go fuck yourself."

Thanks—Chekhov's Darling ready to tune in and please.

Thanks—a genuine one. The most appreciated.

Something tells me Val just used all of the possible meanings concentrated in one.

"I didn't take my vibrator on this trip and good luck to me using fingers and finishing within two to three business days. Let's have something super sweet —not a gesture, a huge cake that we both need right now." I say.

"I missed you, gal." Val smiles.

"Missed me or sanity?" I smile back.

"Maybe both. Let's go on a road trip from East Coast to West Coast," Val says.

"Let's. My new settee delivery has seen more of the US than me," I say.

"We should change that!" Val says.

"Fair warning: if I organize it, we'd tour around America for ten weeks asking different people like politicians, stand-up comedians, and musicians what happiness is for them. We'll have a car dealership for a sponsor, the best Instagram travel influencer to promote the trip, and a production company to shoot the video. So if you want to just go on a road trip, you have to be in charge," I say.

"I kinda like your plan." Val winks.

"Damned! I was hoping to delegate my organizational skills to someone else."

"Was your settee worth the intriguing waiting time?

"Nope," I reply.

"So tell me, Mirra, how can I help you now?" Val

asks as we finish our cakes.

"I need you to lay out carpets of all colors and..."

"...and beautiful necklines for six people?"

"Nah, just one for one," I say.

"To do what?" Val asks.

"To play a Russian roulette and see if we win. Need to change the decision of Sheik Beranger and lower the production of buckwheat. He is a piece of cake."

"Boy oh boy do we love cakes. Is it the kind of sweet cake that makes you squint with pleasure or the one that gives you diabetes?" Val asks.

"It's not going to be easy," I reply honestly.

"If it was, it would've been solved with diplomacy in ties, not naked diplomacy," Val says.

"Yep. I need someone... non-ordinary."

"I have Pavlina—the girl who wears so much shiny lip gloss that even Jessica Simpson in the nineteen nineties wasn't that shiny. She once stopped a fire car in the street. Other than to say she once employed an autistic hacker who she took to a strip club because he was awkward with women. She also keeps chickens as pets in her apartment. And had once been to a Malaysian jail. She had somehow traveled to forty countries for pleasure, and to this day, she keeps avoiding everyone's questions about what she does for a living. During COVID, she flew all over the world and at home at the Belorussian border, when the security asked for her address to track the virus, she kept giving the address of the Head of the Ministry of Internal Affairs—his address was never checked. And she can turn any man into Santa: fat and old who will bring presents. Non-ordinary enough?" Val says.

"Okay, she's crazy. Even her name sounds crazy. Apparently, we need a Belarusian prostitute with gummy bears in her lips. Once again Belarus helps Russia and guards order," I say.

"To the rescue!" Val says and makes the Superman move with my arm up, which makes me laugh loudly.

"It's hilarious," I say.

"Yet true. That's exactly who you need," Val says. "And do I need to know all the whys and motives or my presumptions are enough?"

"Let's just say if your girl manages to help, your governors and businessmen will get back to fucking instead of solving state problems," I tell the truth.

"She'll help you—I have no doubt," Val says.

"How come you're so sure?" I ask.

"Mirra, people hate being excluded, especially billionaires."

Ah, sheik Beranger, the glorious spear...

So it is decided to put a sweaty happiness Pavlina from Mogilev under the decision-making penis in the name of truth and fairness. Sometimes life's not pretty from the front. I guess it really doesn't matter who does things and how if the big-world-ties can't.

Late at night, as I'm staring at the lights of Dubaisk from my hotel's suite balcony in anticipation of at least a yawn, Mason calls me. He always does before something terribly important, I've noticed. Startling.

"Hey. What are the chances I could get a pizza delivered here?" I say.

"Address?" Mason says.

"Tiny blue van at the end of Rape Street. Sounds like a legit USPS address?" I say.

"Hundred percent. If I touch my phone in the right places, a pizza will show up at my door anywhere," Mason says.

"Gentle rough hands Mason. How are you?"

"Recovering from lots of drinking on Fire Island."

"Please don't tell me you were baptized gay."

"Why do people keep saying that?"

"Because, Mister Reeve, you would be a huge loss for the heterosexual testosterone community."

"I have a better idea. Just call it what it is: men."

"The old term is toxic masculinity, duh. Changing the word is supposed to change the attitude, remember?" I say sarcastically.

"Right. I keep forgetting that I'm supposed to be rough but never show it, also be sensitive but be able to kick everyone's ass. So which one is a man supposed to be? Can't be both simultaneously, like eating and pooping: gotta pick one."

Tell a man what he's supposed to be so he will. That is why women like military guys because they know those men can be trained.

"Question of the day: where are you today?"

"In Paris at Harry's New York Bar where Bloody Mary cocktail was created," Mason replies.

By joining the bureau, agents swear to work crazy hours for unfair remuneration, risk their lives sometimes for no reason at all, and proudly wear a metal badge probably made by an underaged in Taiwan. And travel internationally. Sometimes, anytime, lots of time. I can learn geography by pinning places Mason goes to on the map—could be anywhere at any given moment. We talk a lot on the phone and whatnot, about everything and nothing, especially since Franc and I stopped talking. I miss our intellectual stimulation duels with Franc. People are replaceable, sure, but the chemistry is never exactly the same with the others.

My friend Mason Reeve, who sleeps under the dreamcatcher, taught me something obvious I knew and forgot: hurting with words is more painful than being shot—no ibuprofen can help. And I taught him something obvious he knew and forgot: people have to think about their own data trails but also when they are creating data trails for other people, such as when a person uploads their contacts to a technology service—sharing information with the service that those contacts might not want to be shared. Once the data is out there, it can be misused in ways we don't expect.

One thing is for sure: it's common practice for Mason to stand up for me, so I'll always feel like someone has my back. Not in a macho way, just in a way that lets people know they probably shouldn't mess with me. In return I care—that's all he needs. Don't we all?

"Alright, I called to just check in," Mason says.

"I'm good. Thinking about getting a massage. I need a good physical therapist," I say.

"What do you have?" Mason asks.

"Little curve of my spine and stiffness," I say.

"You girls and your curves..." Mason says. "Okay, I'm almost done with my Bloody Mary."

"Go save the world. Cheers to that!" I say.

How nice would it be if all toasts would come true? From A to Z, for all the holidays and get-togethers and celebrations of a lifetime.

NOTHING PERSONAL

Dream big and do something already. I am the initiator of change, the change meant to spread the good energy—the sun energy, so something awesome can happen. I know the rules, but I don't always adhere to them. Sometimes, rules slow down progress and hinder the search for truth. Truth is the criterion, the measure, the meter. Change is always full of polemics, arguments, struggle for new ideas, which is incompatible with timidity and stereotyped thoughts and lack of independence of views. The secret is stamina rather than speed. The right timing is essential and sometimes the best you can do is just wait. As long as it takes, but a few months tops.

I call Val and ask right away: "Did your friend talk to our friend yet?"

"Like, has she been 'hired' today? No," Val replies. "I sent her profile along to the person on his team who is hiring for the position. I will follow up with him today."

"I'm sorry, since when does an escort require a resume and a cover letter?! The whole point was to skip the so-called Human Resources." I flip out a little.

"Unfortunately, that is not how the real world

works sometimes. People have processes in place that they 'formally' follow," Val says.

"Everyone has their own 'real world' just like the news feed on Facebook. Val, you know that," I say.

Val Zironka. Perspicacious, ingenious. She binds intelligence and originality together with genius. Subtlety you can't unfriend. But what the fuck!

Even though NDA is in my DNA, it is incredibly hard to deal with everything all by myself, when I can't even talk to anyone. It's a lonely life so you've got to pick a lot of chess pieces by yourself.

To distract my thoughts from going in the insane direction I watch the stupid reality show *Fixer Upper*. To manage my jitters, impatience, and overthinking, but also because using the vibrator to massage my back isn't enough, I get massages that become the highlight of the week. My physical therapist keeps pressing on my back where the kidneys are, I yell in slight pain and she tells me it's kidney energy: too much thinking results in back pain. "To stop the back pain you have to stop using your brain," she says. I don't drink, I don't smoke, I don't use drugs: I get my high from power and dancing provocatively in a slutty dress in front of a large window in my house. My brain is all I have. Even if I do stop thinking, my boobs won't grow bigger from that. *Ouch! Motherfucker, stop hurting me! I can't stop thinking!* But all I say out loud is "Oy..."

Then she gives me a lecture on the organs and their associated emotions. Heart and small intestine—happiness, joy, excitement, hate, impatience. Spleen, stomach, and pancreas—trust, openness, anxiety, worry. Lungs, skin, and large intestine—courage, sadness, depression. Kidney and bladder—calmness, gentleness, fear. Liver and gallbladder—kindness, anger, frustration. She is the best physical therapist in New York City. She calls herself Grace for the comfort of local idiots in "the best country in the world" who are so stupid they can't even comprehend that people from other cultures have different names given to them at birth by their parents, and for the comfort of arrogant asses they have to have American nicknames. Grace's real name is Ping. What's the limit to which people have to assimilate after immigration?

"It's okay, Mirra. It's okay,' she says. "Next week good, yes?" and hands me my winter coat.

None of the puffers are sexy in a way that society tells us what's sexy, but they are sexy in a comfy grown-up way. I am invisible and faceless in my puffer, which is exactly what's needed—I don't want anyone to recognize me or read my mind. I know, my thoughts might be in such a personalized, coded shorthand that even if someone could read my mind, they wouldn't understand what the heck I'm thinking.

And then there it is. February brings lots of international news. When God wants to punish, he takes away the mind, they say. Everything is upside down in the world as if it were a madhouse and the crazies took over and rule now. Happy hour is sad hour. Bars serve mocktails and bartenders give you a look if you order a cocktail with alcohol. Drug junkies are news junkies consuming mass media like heroin. Magazines issued without Photoshop and new injection medicine creates more wrinkles because old is in trend—the older the better. TV anchors present sub-jective news. People are appreciated for not showing emotions, especially celebrities; and everybody wants to be just like them. Men are objectified and women are praised for being strumpets. All professions are put before names for everyone, not just for doctors and presidents. Face tattoos are business attire. Em-pathy becomes a personality disorder. Doctors pre-scribe social media as a remedy for loneliness. The Department of Labor doesn't provide labor. The No-bel Prize for World Peace is given to those who start-ed at least one war. Authorities arrest loyal friends and handshake with enemies. Broke countries be-come biological and medical waste landfills. Coup d'état is called current festivities. Whisper is loud and yelling is not heard. Mass opinion forms Hollywood movies and Hollywood creates an agenda for the Pen-tagon. Peace foundations sponsor wars. Alcohol pro-duction companies sponsor sports. Non-verbal com-munication prevails over verbal and people barely speak. Everyone knows their bodies and understands their own emotions and the psychology of other peo-ple. A wristwatch is the most valuable thing because it can track time which is as expensive as coal can be. Yes, coal is the new diamond, goes best with the yel-low-gold setting. No one goes on adventures and net-working is condemned. Everyone replies to texts and calls back after a missed call all the time. Old defini-tions are reinvented and new definitions simply suck. Lie is now truth and truth is now lie. And then every-body stops being high and things go back to normal. If only it was that easy. The truth is nothing can go back to normal. Ever. One day I'll write a dark comedy movie "Speechless" about all things in life switched upside down where white is black and black is white and no grey in between, not even one shade. And then a sequel: the imaginary version of the perfect world. I wonder what that is.

Fake-making can be useful when disinformation is meant to distract attention from something specific. It's one of the strategies in war. Why are we at a never-ending war though? Constant duelists end up losing to themselves. But if you don't admit it publicly, it's as if you haven't lost at all, as if going the full length—start with drums and finish with dynamite—you got lucky with not being affected. All news look like failed photos of personality disorders. It's mental.

News 1. "The delegation was unable to fly to the Global Warming Forum due to severe frost and snow drifts," a climate reporter reports. *Climate reporter... Facepalm. I remember the times when reporters could write a story about...wait for it...anything!*

News 2. "Hobby horsing is added as the new sport of the Olympic Games in two categories: lightweight and heavyweight. Russia is banned from sending their team." *Phew. Luckily, there aren't enough distinguished lardheads in Russia to participate in this. Very curious to see the hobby horsing Paralympics.*

News 3. "A social worker comes to a mentally disabled person and jerks him off once a month." *And they say socialism is bad.*

News 4. "AI and business thought leaders share thoughts on differences between humans and AI." *Since when do we care about what AI thinks?*

News 5. "Words *motherfucker, motherfucking* and their derivatives are now added to the dictionary of forbidden words because they are found sexist and biased and offend mothers, fuckers, non mothers, and non fuckers. The new suggested words to use are *their moves towards achieving physical pleasure, their moves towards achieving physical pleasure-ing,* and their derivatives." *So now one word becomes a complex sentence?*

And about the weather, also in propaganda style: "Tomorrow it should not rain again," they say on TV. *Who knows how it really will be? Time will tell.*

An adage stating by Theodore Sturgeon: *"Ninety percent of everything is crap."* All science is based on the phenomenon of constancy. Conclusion: crap is constant ninety percent of the time. And the good ten percent is still very good and is worth fighting for. It needs to be fought for. Be honest and kind—that's all it takes to be a good person. That's it.

So far the world seems to behave like in an old joke: a man went to Monte Carlo to play the Twenty-One card game. When they started talking about who had how many points, someone said: "I have twenty-one." The man says: "Show me." In response: "It's customary for us to take the word for it." And suddenly the man got very lucky in the Twenty-One game.

There are no double standards at all. Double standards is a propaganda fake. There's only one standard: the only one convenient today.

News 1. "To stand up to Russia, these five weapons should be on the wishlist."

News 2. "I'm a weapons editor and here are my

best picks under $50M."

News 3. "Best fashion tricks to use during war."

News 4."A typical mistake at war in your 40s."

News 5."How to entertain yourself in a bunker."

With the Dictionary of Political Propaganda, it is easier to consume the news, like knowing a foreign language proficiently—you understand more.

The government expressed concern about the events: they're not going to do anything about it.

Completely unprovoked action: totally provoked and provocation lasted for years until it reached the non-turning-back point.

This is a threat to democracy: you're making money and we're not getting a cut of your earnings.

Believe me, I'm telling the truth: I'm totally lying, but I want you to believe me anyway.

According to our anonymous sources: oh, we totally made it up.

It needs further investigation: investigation immediately found out who's guilty but is forbidden to announce it publicly.

With all due respect: shut up, idiot!

Peaceful protests: ready to blow out any minute.

We're calling for a thorough independent review: we need more time to cover up all incriminating evidence.

The story is being developed: we haven't received the updated manual on the correct narrative to proceed with, so please bear with us.

Geopolitics revolves around the same menu; diplomacy now is to be able to choose meals from the menu at all.

Menu

Appetizers

Public Condemnation With Trending Hits, Dirt
Digging And Temporary Career Change

Total Reputation Crisis With Canceling On Top

Street Protests With Violence, Arson And Looting

Main courses

Destabilization. Change Of Government, Plain

Change Of Government Revolution Style
*tell the server if you're allergic to blood

Carpet Bombing With Shelling
*goes best with bomb shelters and humanitarian
parole on the side

Dessert

Fervid Democracy Spread On Freedom Crust

Puppet Head With Tantrum And Addiction Mixed
with Country–Sugar–Baby On Allowance

Money Laundering And Resources Restructure

If they broadcast that something is going to happen soon—it already happened.

We are going to blow up the buckwheat pipeline: the attack on the buckwheat pipeline is only a detonation activation button away.

How does the global dollar system work? What is causing de-dollarization? What are the possible effects of de-dollarization on countries, companies, and individuals? Why the de-dollarization might fail: oh, it's already happening, slowly but steadily; you have to go through the denial stage before acceptance.

Generating electricity and heat by burning fossil fuels causes a large chunk of global emissions and climate change: dear partners, we've decided to gretathunberg your economy and sentence your heavy industry and manufacture to death, oops, I mean green energy agenda.

With all the gadgets that we keep inventing, it'd be really useful to have one to meter the level of madness on the news. They could release it as Alexa or an app or simply put it next to the PG-13 sign on the screen. Sometimes, while watching them with peripheral vision, the light from the TV set reflects as if the signal is short-circuited and the matrix glitched. Perhaps it'd also be useful to have a love meter with three options: for friends, lovers, and strangers as a whole to identify the level of empathy towards them as humanity.

No meters, unfortunately, can read between the lines or even more so—between the between the lines. Even in chaos, there is order. And the point is to find hidden order in seemingly random data.

Any type of phobia is exhausting and requires a lot

of energy, effort, and constant repetition of word vomit to maintain—walking on a treadmill of the same information over and over again without a destination point. Anyone trying to appeal to logic, economic impact or, god forbid, have the nerve to object is immediately silenced by a handful of overpriced buckwheat each day. If not—military operations will be broadcast live, like a computer game, with or without a scaffold, metaphorical and whatnot.

Don't switch the channel, stay with us during the commercial break that will only last a moment.

INT. KITCHEN.

COMMERCIAL LADY, close-up of her face. She eats one spoonful of yogurt and swallows it. Her stomach gets covered with flowers and is in the sunshine. Birds are singing, flying around her waist. It is pure happiness after just one spoon of yogurt.

                    COMMERCIAL LADY
            Pasivia created a new un-
            forgettable yogurt: a com-
            bination of berries and
            fruits. Everything turns
            out amazingly thanks to
            it. And any sort of dis-
            comfort is out of the
            question. It is the salva-
            tion for those living an
            active lifestyle and try-

ing to stay healthy every
day.

Close-up. Birds around Commercial Lady
start belly-dancing.

> COMMERCIAL LADY
> New Pasivia has an incred-
> ibly delicate texture and
> a completely new flavor
> for comfortable digestion.
> Mmm...So tasty and
> healthy. Well-being comes
> from the inside.

Medium close-up.

> COMMERCIAL LADY
> New Pasivia. More than
> just a yogurt. It is also
> a furniture polisher.

Medium Shot. Commercial Lady spills one
spoon of yogurt on a table and polishes
it.

> COMMERCIAL LADY
> Just one spoonful of Pa-
> sivia can make your fa-
> vorite wooden furniture
> look all shiny and almost
> like new. No more scratch-
> es or marks ever again.
> New Pasivia. More than

just a yogurt. It is also
a styling foam.

Commercial Lady spills two spoons of
yogurt on her hands and makes up her
hair as if it were a styling foam.

> COMMERCIAL LADY
> Light, non-sticky, holds
> your hair for up to 48
> hours! Fits all types of
> hair, including curly,
> wavy, and straight. New
> Pasivia. More than just a
> yogurt. It is also a snow
> substitute.

EXT. TYPICAL BACKYARD WITH GREEN GRASS.

Commercial Lady with two children near
the pool. FATHER barbecues.

> COMMERCIAL LADY
> Do you live in California
> or Florida and miss the
> snow? Do you feel like
> your kids are missing out
> on making a snowman? Pa-
> sivia can make your family
> snow day the happiest and
> healthiest day of your
> lives.

Commercial Lady spills a lot of yogurt

on the ground. Kids start making a snowman out of it. They are having fun in this yogurt mess.

> FATHER
>> Uh-oh, don't eat yellow snow, guys, only pink snow —it's berries, it's good for you (winks).

> COMMERCIAL LADY
>> With this snow substitute, snowflakes are unique and one doesn't look like the other. New Pasivia. More than just a yogurt. It is also a sperm substitute.

INT. DOCTOR'S OFFICE.

Commercial Lady, who's a doctor now, comes into the doctor's office, PA-TIENT, an old lady, is already there.

> COMMERCIAL LADY
>> New Pasivia is so healthy, so natural and so strong that it can even impreg-nate a woman twenty years into her menopause.

> PATIENT
>> (thumbs up)
>> I'm only 74 and I'm having

triplets! Yay!

          COMMERCIAL LADY
New Pasivia. More than
just a yogurt. It is also
rocket fuel.

EXT. NASA SPACE CENTER, HOUSTON, TX.

          A spaceship is ready to be
          sent to space. There's
          only one thing missing.
          Commercial Lady is on a
          ladder right next to the
          rocket, opens the fuel cap
          and adds two drops of yo-
          gurt using a pipette,
          closes the fuel cap, the
          spaceship goes up to
          space.

          COMMERCIAL LADY
New Pasivia. More than
just a yogurt.

INT. FACTORY.

          COMMERCIAL LADY
Over 30 years ago we
started as a small company
in North Dakota. Our first
revolutionary product was
a 4-color ballpoint pen.

Ever since then, we have
been dedicated to produc-
ing only useful and convenient products for our
customers' needs. If you
like our more-than-just-a-
yogurt, you should check
out our barbecue grill
that's also a family cre-
matory, a watch that's
also a foldable grand pi-
ano, and a can of quick 1-
minute success booster
that's just a can of quick
1-minute success booster.
Because some things are
enough as they are.

And we're back from the commercial break. News, always breaking, take over all the space. Something is going on, I notice, but it makes no sense. It's like the narrator inside my head knows telepathy and can't shut up: talking, talking, talking, talking, talking. It only takes about half a year for the monopolistic media to create the alternative truth.

My team gathers in Teams for a brief talk.

"Guys, who's been creating the Russian phobia narrative in the media?" I ask.

"Probably some fatheads who believe in immortality?" Ian says.

"I'm not crazy—it's the news, right?" Lada says.

"Yeah. It is insane, indeed," Novak says.

"They create the fictitious truth like there's no tomorrow," Triggs says.

"Who the hell are they?" I ask.

"Who the hell knows..." Novak says.

"Which national security slash democracy defendant acronym is it?" I ask again.

"Very possibly all of them," Triggs says.

"We've only been dealing with ridiculous and funny news and actual analysis of real truth," Lada says.

Real truth... Tautology—something I thought I'd never use in a sentence. They are not fake-creating and showcasing just one mishap—it's a systematic long-term strategy against a whole civilization.

I'm gonna have to hug a lot of trees and watch a lot of documentaries about penguins to get over this.

Is the truth on the side of who is stronger or who is right? The truth is not a boat. And even though a boat license isn't required, the person who puts on the captain's cap first is still not the captain. In mass media, whoever blurts out first is right. In social media, whoever yells the most is right. In life, fortunately, this is not the case. Sometimes the truth is too obvious and cannot be hidden, like carrying fire in a plastic bag.

The most important thing for a healthy psyche is a clear conscience. Then suddenly in August:

News 1: "Buckwheat pipeline blast investigation ends but blames deliberate sabotage." *The investigation of the deliberate sabotage that was conducted by the world's best professional investigators, taking into consideration all details of the case, concluded that it was indeed deliberate sabotage.*

News 2: "America begins aid airdrops as talks intensify." *Are they airdropping food or democracy, as always?*

News 3: "Sheik Beranger decides to lower the production of buckwheat." *Let's call it the lucky chance that I asked for.*

Russian diplomat Pal Petrovich and I meet again on the rooftop of the Bureaucratic Obstacles Center, where the opening party on the first day of the International Summit of Lies and Power is held.

"What are you wearing for Halloween?" I ask.

"I'll be in a costume of a Donbass refugee. What are you going to be?" Pal Petrovich says.

"I have a costume of a very tired writer." I shrug.

And we both burst out laughing. It's hysterical.

"Pal Petrovich, I like your ring. What stone is it? Emerald?"

"Peridot," he answers.

"Special ring with a special meaning?" I ask. There's got to be one, otherwise Russians aren't Russians without symbolism.

"When things seem to fall apart around you, it can help you remain calm. Peridot has often been linked to how life tends to unravel in certain cycles and that destruction and rebirth are often two sides of the same coin," Pal Petrovich says.

"You do something, trying to do good, but some things are just pointless. Once, the president of Ukraine gifted a lake boat for freshwater to a prestigious children's camp on the Black Sea—a salty sea. The boat has ever since been a monument on the ground—the monument to pointlessness," I say.

"One who won't try won't find out," he says.

"Remember the fake story that Russians have standing tickets on their planes?" I say.

"Yeah, hilarious," Pal Petrovich says. "It made at least seven countries' representatives at the Bureaucratic Obstacles Center laugh. Wait, was that you?" Pal Petrovich looks surprised.

"Sorry. I had to come up with something..." I smile.

"We're doing it too," Pal Petrovich smiles too.

"Tell me something I don't know..." I say.

"You're doing it with good PR, spreading information globally. We're doing it silently. But we're also doing it. I don't know why we have such bad PR, but perhaps it's for a reason," he says.

Lost in who's *you* and who's *they*, we quietly stare at the Pepsi sign across the East River.

"Indeed 'When everyone is dead, the great game is over. Not before.' The battle's not over. The battle for redistribution of power just started. It's the harbinger of the transformation of the world; the change will be long and painful. I have a premonition that everything will be the new way—it has to be the new way."

Pal Petrovich doesn't even nod—he blinks.

"Wording solves a lot, but money solves more...and usually lasts longer. Until people understand that they need to participate in the life of their country, random people who come to power will do whatever they want," he says.

"Well, someone's going to break under the strain. Money is temporary, but the good is forever." It's my turn to blink.

"Do you love your life here?" Pal Petrovich asks.

"For the most part, yes." *My Ministry of Happi-*

ness has been working steadily lately, compensating for the first few years in a progressive recession of professional needlessness and general loneliness. "Sometimes I miss the openness and friendliness and fast decisions of my compatriots," I reply.

"I've always wanted to move here because I wanted public toilets to have free toilet paper and not a heart-shaped cut in a wooden toilet outside, in the field, in the middle of nowhere. How did you end up here, Mirra?"

"I've been traumatized by Hollywood movies conveying an idea of endless opportunities on the land of people's freedom," I reply.

"Ha. Haven't we all?" Pal Petrovich chuckles. "If you can make it here, you can make it anywhere, they say. They're surely right about that. The country's so not welcoming and treats people so shitty, dividing into classes and groups and checkboxes that if you manage to make it, you're exhausted and done. Only upon moving to the United States do you realize and experience all shades of unimportance."

"Pal Petrovich, you are being very dramatic," I say. The feeling is familiar though. "You know, it's not the territory that starts wars. It's people. People will change, governments will change, the territory will be the same. It's not the territory's fault." I pause and then add, "It gets better if you have an alternative."

"Which one? Coca-Cola instead of Pepsi or Kvas?"

"I don't know. Can I have both?" I say.

"At some point, we all have to choose and stick to one thing," Pal Petrovich says. "I am Russian. I've been listening to American music, eating American food, watching American movies. And now I have an opportunity to have everything my own, everything that I once had, but it was taken away from me with the help of social engineering, which, by the way, I agreed to voluntarily, mistaking not my culture for mine. And now, it's important to take advantage of the opportunity to go back to the roots of my civilization. A chance—the American way."

If you don't start being in charge of your life, someone else will.

Voluntarily or not, that somehow triggers my Ministry of Meanings to open for overtime working hours. It's a dangerous Ministry—a mixture of hope and fear. Fuck, Pal Petrovich! Fuck, fuck, fuck.

"Mirra, have you ever thought about going back home?"

"I am home," I reply looking at the Pepsi sign.

"Don't you ever miss home?" Pal Petrovich continues. "I miss our craziness that no one else in the world seems to understand, moreover to love. We always find a solution for everything in some sort of comforting chaos."

"Pal Petrovich, honestly? I really miss the feeling *mine*: my land, my country, my idea of development. Where I'm going, why I'm going there, what I want from this route in the end, and what I will leave to my descendants."

"Want to go see it again?" he asks.

"I don't even have a visa." I point at the obvious.

"I have a diplomatic passport. And a diplomatic jet. Want to go?" Pal Petrovich looks at me.

"When? Now?"

"Yeah, now. It's only nine hours away."

"That is crazy!" I exclaim.

"Not crazier than what's been going on in the world lately. Right now, the world has the perfect conditions for an escape. We all dream of tuning out, don't we?"

He does have a point.

"Mirra, relax. You won't even have time to get jet-legged. You wanted to feel the spirit again? I'm giving you the opportunity. Take it."

"And what will you want in return?" I ask.

"Geez, Mirra. Nothing," he says like he means it.

"Nothing? It doesn't happen like that," I say.

"It still happens. You're just unaccustomed to normal human relations on a non-commercial basis."

"Didn't you tell me earlier that you were doing it all too?" I say.

"And because we always have that humane component that we can't get rid of, we are often one step behind. We care too much—that doesn't match well with the cynicism of sometimes psychopathic moves on the international chessboard."

He does have a point. Again.

"Fuck it. Let's go! I'll just feel the territory again."

"You'll fly back in three days."

"Back home you meant?"

"Mirra, I meant what I said."

He is worth a good goddamned. It's like I intentionally lose my queen and see how that goes and what happens next and check if I can win this way because this way is more exciting but also easier.

Home doesn't have borders. I think I am done with

this championship. The score is Am 3:2 Ru, but Ru won—the constant paradox of Ru. The world has nothing but to accept it.

Time to see where I'll want to retire.

America is defined by an idea. Russia is defined by a soul.

America doesn"t give a fuck about anyone, and if that's what they call the American dream then I don't want it. Russia only gives a fuck if you know someone and I don't want to have to know someone for the sake of knowing. It's exhausting. I don't want it that way either.

Americans are the most manipulative nation I know. All shows and movies glamorize that too: how to lie and get it your way, sometimes with a bit of comedy. They always have to fake it til they make it instead of just enjoying life and appreciating what they have. They pretend to be someone they are not. Perhaps that is why Americans are so depressed. Russians are like New Yorkers: they don't usually bother you, but if something bad happens—they unite and help one another. They are very nice people. The stereotype is Russians never smile and are always gloomy and angry. True. Russians don't smile all the time for no reason, but once they do—you know for sure that it's genuine.

Russians steel. A lot. All the time. Naebat is a long-time tradition, like Shabbat for Jews. The country must be that reach if there's so much to steel for so long. For Americans, even corruption is available only to a certain privileged class. Boo-hoo!

Most Americans don't have passports—most Russians do. The majority of both can't afford to go anywhere to use their passports.

Americans rename every puppy they see on the street. Russians give nicknames to people they love, as well as to plants and objects, like a fridge.

Both American and Russian doormen can talk to a sparrow in the street and then feed it.

All American women talk with the same annoying intonation, regardless of their accent. All Russian women talk in their own unique way, regardless of their accents. Both American and Russian women are strange creatures: they can be afraid of bees or mice but not afraid to use a sharp eye pencil while driving on a bumpy road.

In America, there are so many attractive men with a six-pack who can't hold a conversation that it's unattractive. In Russia, so many smart men can talk about anything but they are unattractive. Both American and Russian men, if put in one room, will become friends on the basis of simply being men.

American kids in schools don't share test answers with their peers hoping to be the best by putting their classmates down that way. Russian kids share their tests and those nerds who don't—get bullied for being stingy nerds.

Americans have fun naming their businesses: "Havemore" deli, "U Don't Know Nothing Produce," "SMTH ELSE" supermarket. When Russians name their businesses in a funny way, there's always a cuss word hidden in naming, which ends up sounding kind of Chinese.

The most racist white American women usually

have big lips, big butts, and loud voices. If only they understood they look more like black women. Russians say the N-word all the time without implying any negative or degrading meaning to it; they have zero racism towards any race at all.

Americans are afraid to say something wrong in their democratic society. Russians call things the way they are and are blamed for autocracy.

Russians have quite a few morons of their own. Americans have quite a few intellectually compromised [morons] of their own. Each nation has them no matter how you call them.

Americans think that wording is more important. Russians think that how you treat others is important.

Americans throw out food and books. Russians do not.

Americans have electronic map navigation in cars. Russians are guided by the Holy Trinity icons on the car dashboard.

Americans have weird laws like it's a federal crime to sell wine with a brand name including the word "zombie." Russians have weird documents like a Certificate of Being Alive that you have to obtain yourself.

Americans have "Employees have to wash hands before returning to work" signs in public bathrooms. Russians wash their hands without a reminder.

American doctors and nurses wear scrubs outside, including in the dirtiest places like public transportation. Russian doctors and medical workers change into scrubs only upon arriving at their medical offices and hospitals, because the whole point of the uniform is to be sterile and not show off in the street that you know anatomy and can prescribe pills.

In America, parents don't bother putting hats on their babies when it's cold outside. In Russia, parents always make sure their babies are warm enough, sometimes too much overdoing it.

Russia is a very traditional yet very contradictory country. It easily combines Christianity with pagan traditions and superstitions, yet there's no cognitive dissonance. Oh wait, America is the same.

There are no friendships in America. All people care about is money. In Russia, people say "Don't have a hundred rubles—have a hundred friends."

Both Americans and Russians, when drunk, send people sentimental text messages, waking up the next day wincing.

Americans tend to portray people as it fits their rhetoric. Russians tend to dig in and figure out the world from multiple sources.

Russians know that there's propaganda on national television, as well as everywhere else in the world. Americans have no idea they have propaganda too.

America doesn't appreciate the past. Russia doesn't live in the present. Both care about the future a lot.

America's national idea annoys one part of the world. Russia lacks its national idea and that annoys the other part of the world.

In America, everything is loud all the time: TV, radio, ads, air conditioning. Everyone is trying to get heard in a country where being number one is the only acceptable goal. And the loudness war only gets louder, more exhausting, getting straight to your brain. In Russia, success does not necessarily equal how much money one's got. And things are quiet yet everything is accomplished.

Americans love to brag about their superiority and show off. Russians show off even when broke, yet don't brag enough about their actual achievements.

America is known for big shots, flu shots, tequila shots, and gunshots. And the American dream is still being given a shot. Russia is famous for unparalleled hospitality, good-heartedness, shocking compassion and mercy, and fairness. You can momentarily win. But if the moral compass is off, nobody will respect you for your unfair victory.

America is a seething force. Russia is a calm force.

America is about equality. Russia is about fairness. Justice is a legal concept. Fairness is a humane sense. Equality does not imply fairness, but people do not understand this and desperately fight for equality. It turns out that fairness itself is a negation of the principle of equality—the basis of democracy. And what if we need a completely new system for organizing the world—a perfect system where there will be both meritocracy and no discrimination? Where not Amazon's one-day delivery will be valuable, but something intangible yet very expensive. Where consumption will be transformed into spiritual and cognitive orders, the attractiveness of which for consumers won't be limited to just one day. Perhaps all this requires not interfering with each other, and become chummy. America may have better pieces on the board, but chess with the Russians, for whom it's a national sport, is better as a friendly match and not for the sake of a championship.

When Americans say they live in the best country in the world and the world nods along and is like: "Sure, let them think that," it looks like a crazy person at an asylum house who insists he's Napoleon. Explaining American exceptionalism: something has value because most people in the world agree it has value. What happens when they disagree?

Democracy or freedom?

Motherland VS State.

Fairness VS Law.

Past VS Future.

And what to choose for the present?

There's good, very good, and useful stuff to consume, but poetry can be truly perceived only in the native language.

It's the last day of the International Summit of Lies and Power. Mason and I meet in Central Park for a walk on that rare occasion that we both are in Manhattan at the same time. He called.

"Wrote any new poems?" I ask Mason. He is a romantic poet at heart, not meant to be seen by just anyone.

"I have one," Mason says and starts immediately:
> "When I'm alone, I think of her face
> What divine architecture
> A glimpse within
> This compelling design
> Carefully curated, effortless calm
> Sophisticate interpretation
> Of love and awe
> In this infinite storm of beauty

Her strength beyond measure."

"Beautiful," I react.

"Thank you," Mason says. "When you write, do you satire things you love or things you hate?"

"I think satire is meant to make fun of things that are unpleasant, uncomfortable, weird, bad, stupid, cruel, incomprehensible. Satire is meant to help you live through it because whatever you make fun of—disappears momentarily. You don't make fun of happiness," I reply.

I know he wants to talk about something—it was coming—but he does the social dance instead of just getting to the point. So I patiently wait. As we walk near the Jacqueline Kennedy Onassis Reservoir, after a brief silent pause, here it goes.

"Walking on the edge, Mirra..." Mason says.

I lift my hand and point at my ring called *Edge*.

"You don't want to play on that level, trust me," Mason says.

"But I've always wanted to be on that level and play accordingly!" I object.

"The higher it gets the less valuable a human life becomes. Those people have no morals or principles. All they care about is power at all costs, first to get it and then to keep it. It's brutal," Mason says.

"Can anyone perhaps..."

"Outplay them? No. You have to be born that way."

"How can you say that? You work for the government, Mason!"

"I do. But I don't trust the government."

"I get it. There'll always be someone smarter, faster, stronger depending on what's truth today..."

"Truth is fabricated reality based on any state's agenda, you know it," Mason says, pauses, and then nonchalantly adds: "The Russian diplomat is a no-go."

"Are you telling that as a friend or as an agent?"

"Both. Mirra, you don't want to have to choose sides. Trust me."

Oh, protection. Hero instinct.

To illustrate his point he lifts me, makes ten steps forward, puts me on the ground, and walks back to the point where he lifted me, making the distance speak for itself. Point taken. Suddenly, I feel completely powerless, helpless and so small. I used to open doors and get things done. And now...

Hatred will continue to exist in the world, power games will continue to exist in the world until everyone is dead and the whole world, and the whole existence.

What was I thinking? That I can actually change something? With a rubber hot water bottle, vibrator, and toilet brush in my desk drawer? I wasn't the one who put them there, it's not up to me to get them out.

Changing history is never beneficial—history is educational, supposed to help preserve the knowledge from past generations. The goal isn't to make the past okay—it's already messed up. The goal is to be able to live the future as well as you can. Dumbheads do not tend to delve into the peculiarities and historical patterns. One thing I know for sure: what's prestigious is not *to have* but *to be*. It is very dangerous to remain in history as a piece of shit.

Fine. On the merry-go-round, one doesn't get anywhere. Honestly, I don't give a fuck anymore. All fucks were given the past ten years. I'm out of them.

It's time to step away and do only couch politics and kitchen diplomacy. There's so much nothing I have to do. Decisions, decisions...

All this time Mason keeps staring at me in complete silence. This is where I should understand what his silence means, but he either started using Botox or is dead inside—I can't read his face at all. Maybe his eye will blink differently than usual or in a fraction of a second any face muscle will twitch. Nah-ah. Nothing.

"Our timing was always off," Mason says. "Mirrachka, you know we could have..."

"Yeah... We met at the wrong time... Or not. Who knows what might've happened had we actually..."

"Eh... You're right," Mason says. "Damn, woman. You're right...beyond measure."

When people show you who they are, believe them.

"What's going to happen next?" I ask Mason.

"One has to decide what to do: do what they have to do or seek truth. I'll go and continue doing what I was sworn in. You'll go and continue doing what you believe in," Mason says.

"And the world?"

"Mirra, the world operated before you, the world has processes going regardless of you. Just go. Keep going. You're a good writer—concentrate on that."

Ah... Surrender... I look him straight in the eyes. "That's the plan. I'll write screenplays."

"Good," Mason breathes out.

"As much as you love what you do you are so tired

of it," I say and I know I'm right.

Mason nods.

"Maybe it's time for you to teach surveillance or jiu-jitsu or whatnot?"

"Mirra, I can't *not* do what I do," Mason says.

His whole life is about running around and he knows nothing else except it. When not working he's always on the move: biking, cycling, fucking. Without cardio, he is not alive. Perhaps he was running away from something when he started and now keeps running by inertia.

"Maybe I'll have a drink and a cigar and chill for a day," Mason says.

"The FBI and the Bureau of Alcohol, Tobacco, Firearms and Explosives...everything that kills," I say.

"About my voluntold deployment...thank you."

Ah. He figured it out. It is funny: to bribe for someone who can arrest for bribery. Almost like seeking asylum in the country that planted the problem that made you seek asylum in the first place.

"If it's not friends and family and people who love you who help in this life, who else will?" I say.

"Okay, my unofficial work wife," he winks.

"Hey, wanna play chess?"

"What's the point? You Russians always win!"

The bells from the Saint Nicholas Russian Orthodox Church on the Upper East Side start to ring. It's a magical sound.

"You hear that?" It's a good sign," I say.

"Mirra?" Mason looks at me surprised, "Since when do you pay attention to God?"

"With age, you've got to believe in something."

PEACE IS POWER

Hi, I'm Mirra. New Yorker. Thirty-nine years of age. Married, two kids. I don't know much but here's what I know about life so far.

That you can do anything in this world that you want to do. You don't have to do anything in this world that you don't want to do. Just because you can do something doesn't mean you must. Do what makes you happy. It's either you tell people what to do or they tell you what to do. I used to think that way. What if you do what you want to do and people do what they want to do and we don't bother each other? There can be multiple ways, and neither is wrong. Time will tell.

That I don't like changing things a lot: health insurance, face cleanser, physical therapist, and so on, unless they are terrible of course. But even then it takes me an enormous amount of time trying to figure out which one is the new best by reading ingredients and reviews and so on. The same goes for people: unless there are unresolved problems that don't go away so I have to let go, I prefer to stick to the ones I've already chosen and like. However, I do acknowledge that things change, life changes, people change. I changed. For instance, I'm no longer the kind of person that wears Uggs in summer.

That to me, country music is a guy in cowboy boots and a white T-shirt with a two-year-old ketchup stain on it. That's it. I got it! Country is dirty, baby.

That skinny jeans are overrated. A bunch of gay men want all men and women to look like gay men. I want to wear a skirt. And chemise. Perhaps it's insignificant, but now I can be not strong. Also, your jeans should be the least interesting thing about you— Japanese denim isn't a personality. It's cool, but you don't have to tell everyone which city in Okayama they came from—stop it.

That before people took lots of pictures of everything so it's well documented for museums to exhibit. Today people take lots of selfies. Oh god, what are we going to see in museums soon? Naked asses and duck faces with brows covering half of the body? Let's just microblade brows on the ass cheeks and be done with this Brezhnev obsession.

That Stillwell Avenue absolutely has to be at the crossroads of Yetbad Street, with Haha Drive ahead and Happy Place leading to a Dead End Road. And Love Lanes throughout the map, please.

That psychopaths are not hired for intelligence work—number one rule. Interestingly, one of the strange characteristics of psychopaths is their choice of pets: they are almost never cat people, because cats are willful.

That back in the day, people said less shit because of duels.

That before thirty I didn't even understand when

people said they had problems. Problems? Huh? What? And now I get it. It's like you can't understand the definition of this term until you get a few wrinkles on your forehead. That's the way nature programmed you. After thirty you can't say you're not ready for anything. Sure, you might not be ready for death but you had three decades to figure stuff out. So, you're ready!

That I'm not responsible for other people's feelings, in most circumstances. Their emotions are their own. Drama makes me tired and I have better ways to spend my energy on; no bridges need to be burnt unless absolutely necessary and strategically planned.

That less random things are funny and more are philosophical; when they are funny—they are hilarious and not just ha.

That right or wrong is not about the majority—it's about the truth.

You live—you learn.

When you're playing the chairs game trying to sit on two chairs with one butt, everyone sees you're playing the game and at the end of it you get none of the chairs.

It's important to make the right choice. Everyone has their own one to make—sometimes it's a choice of a lifetime. Yet, I still have a few questions unanswered.

Is it power that ruins a person or a person that ruins power?

Is it better to live better or to live honestly?

What to choose: Russian soul, Chinese wisdom, American dream, or Jewish luck?

What is freedom really? I am free and thus there can be no vileness towards me or I am free and thus I can cause any type of vileness?

Can the navel become untied?

And finally, who put the rubber hot water bottle, vibrator, and toilet brush in my office desk drawer?

There are times when it's important to know how to live with unanswered questions.

So I'll never find out about those three objects in the drawer, because I am neither in a hurry nor am I on a tight schedule, reconforming, thriving in a fast-paced, rapid-response environment.

No proven track record as a communications and press expert, leader, and manager, with extensive experience in working with principals and brands on executive communications strategies.

No relationships and experience working with top-tier local, state, and national reporters and outlets, such as The Blah Blah Times, Fortune Cookie, Norbes, IDENTICO, Leeafberg, The Washandgo Post, LNN, ACBC, ACDC, Charades Press, The Floor Avenue Journal, Shreuters, and more.

No ability to translate complex fiscal and policy information into clear, compelling language and curate content across all channels to connect with various audiences and the public at large.

No strong written communication skills, including both writing and editing for concise communications.

No creative presentation and visual skills, including graphical and data visualization abilities.

No working knowledge of graphic design and ability to direct and manage individuals responsible for design layout for print.

Don't want all that anymore. I'm over it. My time is only my time now. I started prioritizing and became fussy with what I spend my time on.

Nothing has to be difficult so you appreciate it more. Everything can be easy. And it should. You don't have to strain yourself to live happily. For some reason, there's a belief that you have to eat shit before becoming somebody, to acknowledge your value. No, you don't. You are already somebody—you are you.

First, I was so afraid to get lost in a man, then I was afraid to get lost in my work. Now, tired of all the whores, political, metaphorical, and whatnot, I'm not afraid of anything at all.

Sometimes I felt like I was a horse on the track that ran in a circle, sometimes the horse stood at the start waiting for the race to finally begin soon, now the horse walks freely on the lawn and...in fact, it is no longer a horse, but a happy ginger cat enjoying the sunshine.

As it turns out, I'm a perfect homebody. I love my house with the water view and the surrounding area, which I may not leave at all for days. And I'm cool with that. No longer running around with the eyes of a pooping cat is needed, no hustle and bustle, or even the sound of the city that never sleeps. I've outgrown all of it. The best time is spent in my own nest, my hearth that I created and I'm loving it.

I don't have to wake up super early in the morning and go to work. Instead, I can wake up at any time. I don't even want to be sitting in front of a computer—I don't enjoy it unless I'm writing. Swap screens for scenes, baby! Instead of consuming content—produce content in the form of an in-person conversation, inspire a stranger in the street, spread the sun energy by genuine smile and love. I walk with love by having it tattooed on my ankle. No, it does not mean miso soup. I checked. When people ask me what the tattoo means I answer that it's the most important thing in life. And right away they guess what the most important thing is. Quite interesting to hear. Love is never number one in their guess list.

All I like now are the simple pleasures that have lasted for centuries all over the world: talking to people, because everyone has a story and it's unique; being in nature more, because for my asphalt generation getting back to the basics is fulfilling; and my specialty—pickled watermelons. I'd pickle fairness to make it stay for as long as possible.

Each day I grow my garden, I grow my children and I grow myself as a better person.

A human being needs community, purpose, identity to have meaning in life. Today, identity has become brand, lover has become partner, friendship has become network—person has become corporation. Brands compete with what really matters; we easily give out the important things in exchange for Amazon Prime. I want to have an identity, not a brand. My own iPhone thinks that me from ten years ago and now are two different people and shows me me as two separate people in the Photos app. Speaking of identity... You might not recognize me, you stupid AI algorithm, nonetheless it is still me. That is exactly why robots will never take over.

In the era of all tech, when even car manufacturers have forgotten the primary purpose of a car—to get from point A to point B—not to be a tablet, it's important to maintain digital well-being.

Digital hygiene, digital veganism, detox mode. Here's the toolkit: Delete.

That was a great era when people looked at each other and not at their phones. Grandma Mirra misses that era. I still live there mostly. No social media. I don't care what people eat, how big their asses are, where they go on vacation, or the political opinions of people I went to high school with.

A human being is designed to eat meat (look at the teeth), while smartphones aren't our natural survival tool, although they have already become one to some people. Having a phone is a temptation to stop thinking and start consuming. By freeing yourself of that, free time is spent on thinking. You'll have time to hear yourself thinking. And oh boy do I like thinking!

It used to be a pill for everything—now there's an app for anything. Two hundred and ninety-seven open tabs and eighty-three applications on the phone. I was spending so much time and energy on managing my online accounts, storing passwords, changing passwords for security reasons, and getting distracted by emails I never signed up for. Analytics, metrics, conversions. It's too much! Too much stuff, ads, options. Show Reader for all web pages is the only way to handle it. It has to be fast though, before an annoying email sign-up form pops up and then again in a minute and again as you read the information you came for in the first place. I can't.

Dear Mirra,

In response to your request to delete your account, we regret to inform you that accounts cannot be deleted, they can only be deactivated.

If you would like to deactivate your account, kindly reply to this email within the next twenty-four hours with all the following information so that we can confirm your identity and consider your request:
– Your first name and last name (as entered when you created your account): ....
– The User ID of your account: ....
– The email address associated to your account: ....
– Your date of birth in day/month/year format (for instance 11 January 1980): ....
– A copy of your ID card or passport page showing your full name, nationality, and date of birth. This document is required for your request to be considered.
Thank you for your understanding.

Best Regards,
Unite Service Desk
24/7 Global Support for Key Internet Nonsense Systems Incorporated

It took me a few weeks to delete most of the accounts: Adopets, Altice, American Express, Audacity, Audacy, Canva, Ceridian, Chownow, Converse Dayforce, Delta, Demandforce, Doordash, Emerald, Fcb, Gmmb, Goldman Sachs, Goodshepherds, H&M, HireArt, Icims, Indeed, Interpublic, Jobs-we-worldwide, Josie Maran Cosmetics, L'oreal, MailChimp, MediaBistro, MSG Entertainment, Nebula Genomics, PaidMemberships, Pawslikeme, Paycomonline, Pernod Ricard Group. PetPro Connect, Princeton, Sapsf, Smile Cafe Dental Spa, ShopRunner, SuccessFactors, Taleo, ToutVendre, 23andme, ThemesKingdom WordPress, Ultipro, Upwork, Vimeo, WarnerMediaGroup, Wise. And the big ones: Amazon and Google. A hundred accounts. I also deleted all discount and loyalty cards—they all are useless clutter. No accounts, besides essentials. Email me so I can ignore it easily. If it's important—call. If you don't have my number—that is the answer.

I unsubscribed from all email notifications and they sent me another email notifying me that I unsubscribed. *Bitch, I know! Stop notifying me! I am free now.*

Digital footprint paused—actual footprint resumed.

So I created a Use Less Day on November thirteenth. Less plastic, less stuff, less processed foods too. The farmer's market is the best. Dylan is turning into a quarrelsome old lesbian about it. But what other option does he have really? Divorce me? Hahaha.

Decluttering both online and offline is important, so you don't spend any more time managing physical stuff and digital nonsense—instead, you can spend your time together with your loved ones. We believe that buying more will help resolve a made-up dilemma. In reality, we already have enough precious crap. It makes more sense to take people you love with you as you keep going. Things are easily replaced whereas some people aren't. You can't order a relationship on Amazon.

I even deleted the calendar.

App for things, app for people, app for experiences. Productivity apps made me the least productive; relying on technology, I couldn't remember anything I had to do. After having deleted all of the apps I rely on my own brain for calendar and counting and remembering things. My natural processor works just as well, even better.

No calendar is required to remember to do what I like: play drums for instance. My garage is also my rehearsal room for when I play drums. Dylan laughs that since any business in America starts in a garage, something might happen at my idea center again. In response, I don't deny it. Who knows? Better no though. I just don't want to be tired all the time again and be busy all the time again and in general erh. Knowing me anything can happen, obviously. For now, I'm slowing down. I say so but nothing is ever good for extended periods of time. It gets too hot, too cold, too lonely, too crowded, too much, barely enough...

Traveling used to be great until it became not anymore. Constantly moving without stopping and feeling uncomfortable in crowded places to recreate what exactly? No thanks. I have people I like in my place, my people, and I'm not moving. Besides, it took me a while to get here. More often than not I was uncomfortable in a controlled environment, thinking that getting out of your comfort zone is how you evolve. No. You do need your comfort. Getting out of your comfort zone is not evolution—it's survival; and surviving all the time is, oh my god, exhausting. You see, you learn, you enjoy. That's about it. You don't make an impact and create by being on the move—you create by staying in one place.

Each person needs something to do, someone to love, and somewhere to go. Occupation, love, route. Almost like the holy trinity.

At almost forty years old I am a stay-at-home mom, a stay-at-home full-time writer and that's pretty much all I do. I no longer do any of the cool things in New York City but it's nice to know I could. Stability now equals creativity. I am enjoying my mundane boredom a lot—my balance.

Money and education allow people to venture farther, without needing to rely on relatives for child care or a place to sleep. But that freedom sometimes goes hand in hand with isolation—another false type of freedom that is supposed to be fulfilling and meaningful. Self-sufficiency is difficult and expensive. I gave up that "freedom" voluntarily and that brings a tremendous amount of joy in my life.

The aha moment: I can do whatever the hell I want, which, technically I always did anyway, and now even more so than ever. After I have figured it out and hit the imaginary mail on the head with that statement, I am officially impressed with life.

Life is multidimensional, love is multidimensional, but you only have one route. Sure, you'll get distracted from your route or from what you think is your route, but then you eventually do what you're supposed to do.

I want to live and not bother. And write.

Oh, I love writing more than anything! When I sit down and open the Pages app it's like I get lost in another dimension—I create the other dimension. The reality on the screen can be anything I imagine, and then it becomes life. With paper, it's almost like I know the secret of making dreams and wishes come true. You're welcome to use it. It's not a secret. Enjoy.

At least one more book is on hold— love stories of all people I know; real-life entertaining content, from the most annoying things of humankind to the most precious moments. There's nothing bigger than love. I'll dedicate the book to the love of life. Until then I have to finish the current novel that will most likely be banned in the United States. And I have an idea for a new satire book.

Eight titles of my own, five ghostwritten memoirs, a mini-series show on a streaming service: how is that not enough for an occupation? I am a professional writer. And I've got nothing to prove anymore.

The road wasn't smooth at all. At some point, I considered stopping writing for good. It did bother me that things weren't moving as fast and successful as I expected—things weren't moving anywhere at all for a very long time; becoming famous and acclaimed was probably off the table. I will never forget what my

Ma told me.

"Answer this: how many days a week do you write down your thoughts in the Notes app?" Ma asked.

"Every day," I replied.

"Then you won't be able to stop. You need to write otherwise you'll be miserable and will explode with thoughts," Ma said.

"I don't know, Ma, I guess..."

"A lot of talented people, who are now famous, got their breakthrough around forty years of age. I am certain you will be a widely known and read writer."

"Oh, stop it. You're just saying it because you're my Ma."

"I'm saying it because I believe in it."

"Fine. I won't quit," I say. *What other option do I have? Pity myself and suffer? Already tried that and it still didn't land me a publishing contract.*

Since then I've grown enough to realize that Ma always ends up being right. Wise woman.

The best appreciation an author can get is when her book is read in the bathroom. Hope my words and stories are enjoyed in toilets around the globe.

I've dreamed about owning a business and there was the right time to make it a reality, and I did—I scratched my entrepreneurial itch. Silently, I've dreamed about working for the government and I did, even beyond—I scratched that itch as well. Within only ten years my life went from a typical Tinder non-sense message "Hey gorgeous, so would you want to smoke a joint and make out sometime?" to an IT startup to playing at the world geopolitics map. Now I'm settled and just write books—exactly what I've always wanted. My dream now is to sell one million copies. It's not about the money—I have money, way more than enough for a chill, calm, comfortable life. One million copies sound like a good number to brag about—legit. I don't know why I'm stuck at this number, perhaps because this is what I made at the consulting firm yearly, after tax, so I can comprehend it?

The absurdity of the publishing industry is that even after leaving a footprint in the world events, I still dream about selling a million copies of my books.

> "Oh Time!
> The moving mirror of eternity!"
> © Fyodor Tyutchev

Time started to fly. You wake up in the morning, you have your cup of coffee, you do something and then bam! It's already three o'clock in the afternoon and bedtime soon thereafter.

Life is like an airplane flight.

Being a kid is preparing for the flight, packing, buying tickets.

Teen years is getting to the airport on time in traffic—intense.

Twenties—being inside the plane but still on the ground, taxing towards the right runway.

Thirties—you're on the right runway, speed to the maximum, and go as fast as you can to finally take off.

Forties—you're up in the sky, chilling in first class or sweating in the middle seat in the middle row in economy class. Typically, this is an indicator of how your twenties and thirties went; although, there are of course ohmygodable exceptions. Occasional turbulence equalizes all seats in all classes, but the flight goes smoothly.

Fifties—the flight is on time or maybe a few minutes late. Yes, you can add more speed while already flying but usually you go as is, without the extremes.

Sixties—getting ready for descending. It's slow but steady. You feel it. You buckle up not because you need that extra safety (it doesn't matter anymore), but because at this point it's a habit. Some land faster than expected. Some even make it on the news reporting on their landing. For most, it might take a while, up until eighties or even nineties, if lucky.

I think about the future a lot.

Making a choice is sometimes difficult and not at all like it used to be in your twenties. Now there's way more to consider mixed with less fucks given. And more often than ever, if you can't decide something— put it on pause and "samo rassosetsya" It'll be resolved on its own, somehow, anyhow. And if not— you'll take it off pause and deal with it. Sometimes, making a choice means stepping into the broad spectrum of adventure or stepping out of it—either one is terrifying in some instances.

Also, it is incredibly hard to plan. The threshold for planning in the USA is retirement, even if you are twenty-six at the moment. I am from another part of the world. My planning threshold: a month, well, a year at most. And then we'll see. Moreover, I still don't know in which country I want to retire.

Dylan and I are sitting in our living room watching the sunset. Lame, I know and I apologize, but that's the reality I've chosen.

"Want a joke?" I ask Dylan.

"Always," he says.

"In Central Park, I saw an addict on a bench cooking dope. And they say New Yorkers don't like to cook and always order delivery. Oh, here's another one: junkie in a park cooking dope. It was heroin, and compared to all the imported generic stuff, he was basically using organic whole food drug.

"When did you write the jokes?" Dylan asks.

"Just now, right in front of you."

"Mirra, you should do stand-up."

"Dylan, you're a third person who tells me that."

"What?! I'm not your number one person?" he smiles.

"It's funny how some things change: I used to be afraid of stage. Not only have I overcome the fear of public speaking, now I almost crave it. Besides, I've succeeded at doing creative stuff that pays nothing, might as well add another activity to that list."

"Mirra, don't dramatize. Your writing does bring decent income."

"Yeah, but this is not enough and there's always room for more. Am I being taught in schools to kids?"

"You curse in your books! Not exactly PG-13."

"Henry Miller also wasn't a prude in his writing."

"You can teach a writing course." Dylan knows how to curb my nagging and turn it into the right flow.

"Talking about writing? Hmm...interesting," I say.

"Who did you want to be as a kid?" Dylan asks.

"Ha! I always said I wanted to be Petrosyan. He was a very famous Russian stand-up comedian at the time. Who did you want to be?"

"The two-star general. Don't laugh." It's too late.

"Should I get you another neon sword to fight the imaginary enemy, General Dylan Goode?" I ask.

"My army is winning under my guidance, duh... And I haven't broken the old sward yet," he laughs.

"Oh, I got it!" I keep producing ideas. "I can combine satire and philosophy, open a YouTube channel 'Naked Mind', cause nudity always sells, and comment on stupidity in daily news..."

"There you go." Dylan looks glad he planted an idea in my head.

"I even have videos of two high-ranking officials from two parts of the world saying the exact same sentence, which once again proves that Americans and Russians have more in common than they think or want or are willing to admit," I say.

"What's the sentence?"

"*What a stupid son of a bitch.*"

"Fun. What do you want to do next?" Dylan asks.

"Volunteer at an older community.

Mentor someone young,

Adopt a kid.

Learn ballroom dancing. I want to dance with you more. Where did the slow dance go? Can someone please explain why our society rejects it?

Be an extra in a movie.

Bake a cake.

See the northern lights.

Meet someone I can only dream of meeting.

Write a movie script about AI that appears in a Russian village where it learns the real delights of life and how to feel; become a member of the Writer's Guild of America. I know those two things are self-excluding, but one can dream, right?

Maybe have short hair again—my short cut adds to my sophisticated demeanor.

Create a no-loneliness club OkStranger. Lots of people have problems simply because of a lack of communication. Help them meet each other and talk to each other more.

Fly first class to Australia and Alaska, visit Baikal.

Handwrite a book in a Moleskin notebook and sell it for $19,000 as a rare collectible book, that it will be one day.

Publish a satire magazine "Deskat".

Plant trees and watch them grow for years.

Ride on the swing. I love that feeling of excitement: catching your breath, higher, higher! More! It's scary, but you do it anyway.

Arrange jam sessions with musicians. It is incredibly inspiring and uplifting.

Meet with friends more often to have a good time. After all, it's so cool to sit, reminisce, and say: 'We had such a good time...'

And many more things I can't think of right now. I haven't tried so many things in life."

"Mirra, I meant what do you want to do next like watch a movie maybe?" Dylan smiles.

"Oh, sure, let's watch something for escapism, not realism. So, from the nineties? Those movies are the best," I say.

"Tell me a new password—gotta reset our Netflix," Dylan says.

"Same as you had?"

"Sameasyouhad?" Dylan types. "Capital S?"

I laugh. "Sure. Or type Mirraisawesome!"

"Too late, babe. And nice list. Write it down for me so I don't forget what to get you for your birthdays, will ya?" Dylan says.

"And one more thing: we should make you a Russian passport," I say.

"What for?" Dylan looks surprised.

"So you have it and I won't have to choose."

One thing I know for sure: what's important comes not from the pocket, stomach, and crotch, but from the soul, heart, and mind.

Politics, music, humor.

Without strategy, you can't create anything.

Without laughter, your "cuckoo" can go south.

Without melody, all is boring, and how not to dance when your soul is singing?

AUTHOR'S NOTES

sits in office
bare ass.
past stuff. (here?)

Group chat
explanation of
bare ass

Oh, I'm sure they
already calculated
this probability.

meets homeless guy

buckwheat plan
(what is the plan?
and reveal in what
chapter?
but someone has to inform
Russia about what's coming.

Summit 5days
cocktails.
team presentation
(HARACTERS!)

World Bar
Pal Petrovich

Apricot Jam DAY 1
　　　　　Sept. 29.
Mason convo live

voluntold
　　deployment.

past stuff move here?
make present?

~~mmmmmmmmmm~~

↗ Dylan convo

↘ Mason convo live

~~mmmmmmmm~~

Reveal why those 5 weird
thing in work desk

DC trip Laos
posters
or where October
snova past? 14?

character develop.

Dubaish trip
Val   November?

Maron Convo Call
      Rape Street.

срас в период Dec-Jan
all upsid down
speachless
взорвали Петропавл February
Пропагандопр-вод
Тоже взорвать?

summit 1 year later
September

Rooftop convs
правда

Rus dip.

Trip to Moscow

PLAYLIST

1. Oleg Adjikayev "Guitar House Blues Jam"
start page 7 I am sitting in the office with my ripped...
end page 11 Parliament, as a live group chat, is not...

2. Lube "Ulochki Moskovskie"
start page 61 Orange-the color of happiness...
end page 62 Funny enough, some Hollywood movies...

3. KC & The Sunshine Band "Shake, Shake, Shake"
start page 69 But thanks for the "additional guarantee"...
end page 70 At the hotel restaurant, where we are...

4. Polyphia "Ego Death"
start page 83 And then there it is. February brings lots...
end page 87 Geopolitics revolves around the same...

5. Dmitri Shostakovich "Russian Waltz"
start page 102 Time to see where I'll want to retire...
end page 107 And what to choose for the present...

6. Toto "Hold The Line"
start page 131 And one more thing: we should make you..
end page 131 ...when your soul is singing.

Listen on https://www.youtube.com/@writermilkova

ghostwriter

PRODUCING CREATIVE PROJECTS.

II

All good books are alike—after you are finished reading one you will feel that all that happened to you and afterwards it all belongs to you: the good and the bad, the ecstasy, the remorse and sorrow, the people and the places and how the weather was.

© Ernest Hemingway

mi1.club
+1 917 719 0794
dearMI1club@gmail.com